Return
Please re
Items
req

To Mum, For continuously helping me to solve life's mysteries. Love always, Claire x

To Claire's mum, who I haven't met but sounds very nice. Alasdair

This is a work of fiction. Names, characters, places and incidents are either the product of the author's imagination or, if real, used fictitiously. All statements, activities, stunts, descriptions, information and material of any other kind contained herein are included for entertainment purposes only and should not be relied on for accuracy or replicated as they may result in injury.

First published 2023 by
Walker Books Ltd
87 Vauxhall Walk, London SE11 5HJ

2 4 6 8 10 9 7 5 3 1

Text © 2023 Alasdair Beckett-King
Illustrations © 2023 Claire Powell

The right of Alasdair Beckett-King and Claire Powell to be identified as author and illustrator respectively of this work has been asserted in accordance with the Copyright, Designs and Patents Act 1988

This book has been typeset in Adobe Garamond, Caveat, ITC American Typewriter, Fjalla One, Dina's Handwriting, Uncle Edward, Burbank and Blogger Sans.

Printed and bound by CPI Group (UK) Ltd, Croydon CR0 4YY

British Library Cataloguing in Publication Data:
a catalogue record for this book is available from the British Library

ISBN 978-1-5295-0104-9

www.walker.co.uk

MIX
Paper | Supporting
responsible forestry
FSC® C171272

WALKER
BOOKS

MONTGOMERY BONBON

MURDER AT THE MUSEUM

ALASDAIR BECKETT-KING
ILLUSTRATED BY CLAIRE POWELL

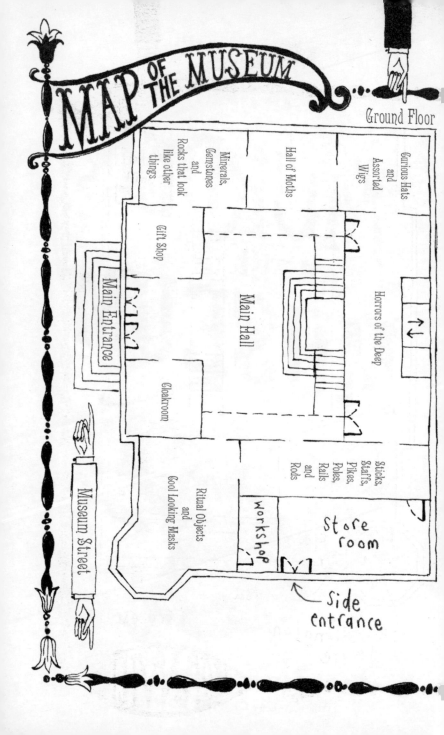

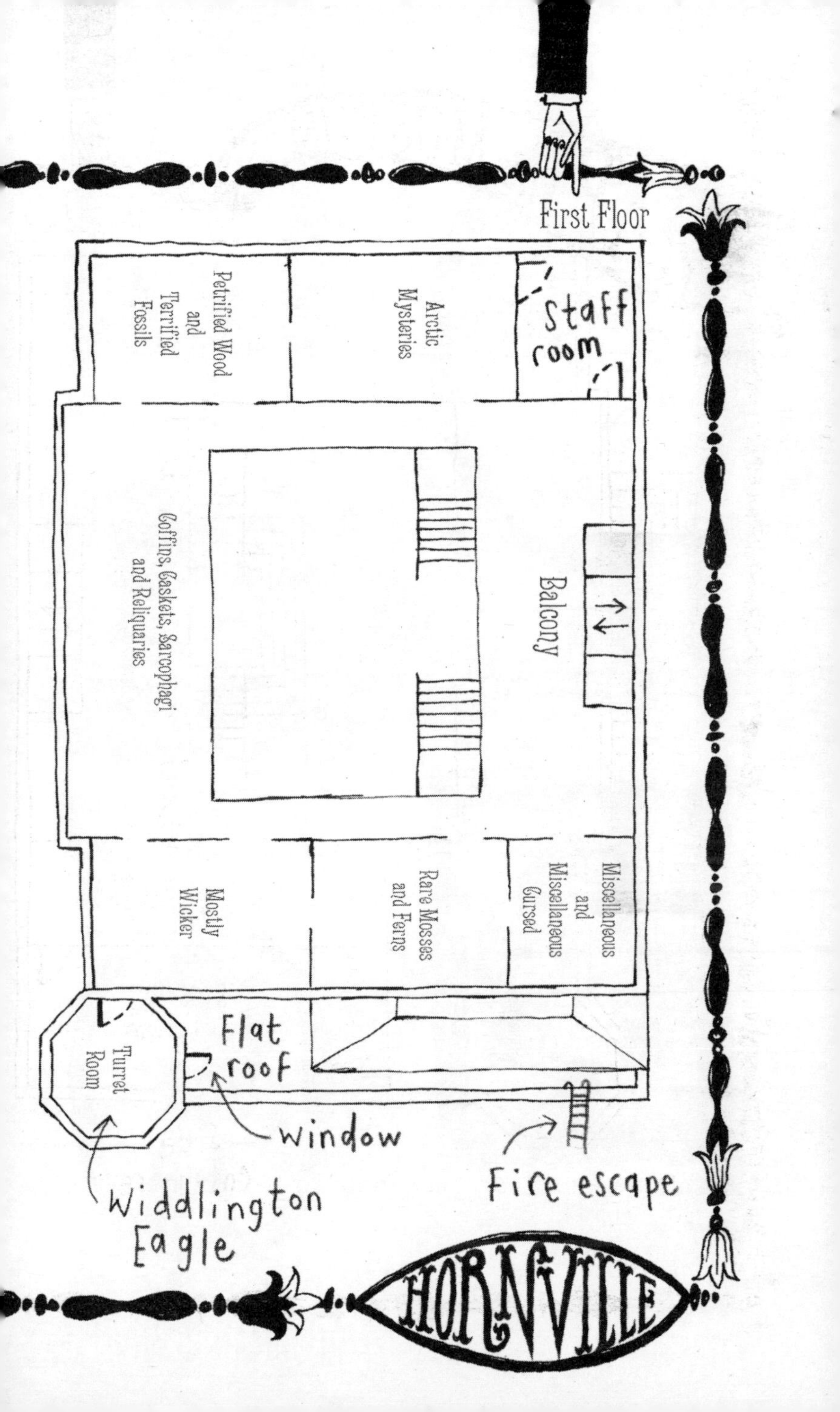

First Floor

Petrified Wood and Terrified Fossils

Arctic Mysteries

Staff room

Coffins, Caskets, Sarcophagi and Reliquaries

Balcony

Miscellaneous and Miscellaneous Cursed

Mostly Wicker

Rare Mosses and Ferns

Turret Room

Flat roof

window

Widdlington Eagle

Fire escape

HORNVILLE

BONNIE
MONTGOMERY

GRAMPA BANKS

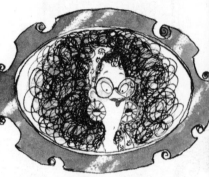

LIZ MONTGOMERY

DANA
HORNVILLE

HERMAN HORNVILLE

· RASHIDA ZAKI ·

ABELARD HORNVILLE

INSPECTOR SANDS

HARRIET SPRUCE

WARBOYS

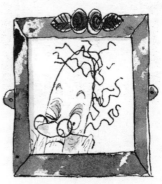

ANTON PRICE

Chapter One
Bonnie

It always seemed to be dusk inside the Hornville Museum. Even in the bright days of summer, it remained chilly and dark – like a fridge dropped down a mineshaft. The narrow windows were blackened with soot, dating back to the years when Widdlington was a town of coal fires and steam locomotives. Hundreds of glass cabinets looked like they had been cleaned only slightly more recently than the windows. Everywhere, signs read: **STRICTLY <u>NO</u> FLASH PHOTOGRAPHY**, a warning that the museum exhibits had got used to never-ending twilight, and that was the way they liked it.

Bonnie Montgomery was the youngest person the Hornville had seen in a long time. The museum reminded Bonnie of the discount aisle in the local supermarket, piled high with bizarre bargains that nobody really wanted: cruel weapons, whalebone carvings, strange grinning masks, and some suspiciously cheap lawn furniture. She had been begging Grampa Banks to bring her here for ages, and she was not disappointed.

The museum's full name was the Hornville Museum of Natural History and Suchlike, and it was supposed to be the oldest building in Widdlington. Bonnie thought this was a pretty funny way to go about things: putting a museum in the middle of nowhere and hoping a town would come along later. But everything about the Hornville was pretty funny, especially the bizarre creatures that loomed over its visitors. She pressed her nose against a glass case in front of her, staring up at a terrible, snarling creature, frozen in the moment of death.

"Did you know they call them Hornville's Monsters?" she asked Grampa Banks in a hushed museum voice.

Grampa Banks was reading a brochure and noisily eating a lemon sherbet. He always brought lemon sherbets when he took Bonnie on a day out, and he always pretended he was not going to let her have one, which they both found hilarious. Grampa Banks was the sort of person who enjoyed museums by plodding methodically from exhibit to exhibit, reading every brass plaque and muttering, "Mmm."

Bonnie preferred to follow her instincts, darting from case to case whenever something shiny caught her eye. She was never looking for "Mmm"; she was looking for "Aha!" This was what made them such an excellent team.

Summer holidays with Grampa Banks were always fun, even when they did not involve murder. (Today *was* going to involve murder, but Bonnie did not know that yet.)

Hornville's Monsters were like no animals you would ever see at the zoo. Reading from his brochure, Grampa Banks explained to Bonnie that someone named Abelard Hornville, a man with a huge fortune and an even bigger beard, had bought Widdlington

Museum in 1931 and stuck his name on it. Old Hornville was a self-taught archaeologist, an amateur palaeontologist and an enthusiastic naturalist. He was also the kind of person who never bothered reading instructions. So, when explorers sent him the bones, skins and tusks of exotic and extinct animals, he assembled them in whatever way took his fancy. A trunk here, a fin there, a couple of beaks… He stitched them together, stuffed the poor beasts full of sawdust, and put them on display.

Tourists flocked to see the sabre-toothed bat, the diplodingo and the mighty flamingopotamus. Meanwhile, Hornville became a laughing stock in the scientific community – until everyone remembered how rich he was, and shut up about it.

Bonnie stared into the cold, hard eyes of a chimpanzebra. She could not escape the creeping sensation that the creature was staring back at her.

"Can I have a lemon sherbet now?" she asked.

Grampa Banks grinned. "Nope, they're all for me."

"Aw!"

That was when the lights went out.

With a *poomf!* the museum was plunged into pitch-darkness. Bonnie felt Grampa Banks grip her hand as startled shrieks and cries of alarm echoed around the Hornville's vaulted halls. The grimy windows let in so little light, they might as well have been auditioning to be walls.

"Did you hear that?"

"What's happening?"

"Someone spat a lemon sherbet at me!"

Then came the scream.

And what a scream it was. A rattling, terrible, bone-chilling scream from somewhere on the floor above.

The anxious museum visitors fell instantly silent, and Bonnie felt Grampa Banks squeeze her hand even tighter. The only light was a sickly green glow from a single fire exit sign, and it cast crooked, dancing shadows all around Bonnie; shadows that seemed to have claws and teeth.

Something, thought Bonnie, is afoot.

Many people go their whole lives without noticing anything that is afoot, amiss or even untoward: without ever experiencing that toe-tingling, tummy-twisting sensation that a mystery is about to unfold. Bonnie Montgomery noticed things that were afoot all the time because, unlike most ten-year-old girls, she was the world's finest detective. This fact was known only to Bonnie herself – and Grampa Banks. Even Bonnie's mum did not know. This fact was a secret because ten-year-old girls are not allowed to be detectives. And they are certainly not allowed to solve murders, because murder is frowned upon.

Bonnie was a great detective, even though she had never *officially* solved a case. A mysterious gentleman known as Montgomery Bonbon, however, had assisted the authorities on numerous occasions. Montgomery Bonbon could not be reached by telephone, and nobody knew where he lived. All they knew was that he was an unusually short man with a shabby old raincoat, a big, bristly moustache, and an accent that was very hard to place.

While Bonnie was on a school exchange trip to Switzerland, it was Bonbon who unmasked cheese billionaire Mandrake Lesuisse as the Emmental Bandit. When the Rusakova Ballet came to Bonnie's home town, it was Bonbon who restored the Rusakova diamonds to the person Countess Rusakova had stolen them from. And when Bonnie visited the Widdlington Wildfowl Park, it was Bonbon who busted an international owl-smuggling ring, resulting in the arrests of over twelve owls.

Bonnie felt Grampa Banks gently loosen his grip on her hand. Both of them knew that Montgomery Bonbon was needed in the Hornville Museum today. The darkness was like a black velvet curtain drawn around her as she transformed into the renowned detective. She did not need a mirror; she had done this many times before.

First, she unzipped her backpack and pulled on his old raincoat.

Second, she tugged her beret down at a jaunty angle that implied a keen and inquisitive mind. She was already wearing the beret, of course. Whether you are a ten-year-old girl or a mysterious foreign gentleman, you still look good in a beret.

Finally, she produced a sticky false moustache and pressed it into place on her upper lip – giving it a few wiggles to make sure it was secure.

Then she threw back her shoulders and took a deep breath.

Bonnie Montgomery had become Montgomery Bonbon.

BONBON THROWS BIG CHEESE IN COOLER
JAILBIRDS! LOCAL SLEUTH CRIES FOWL
"JEWEL NEVER BELIEVE IT!" P.I. Puts Diamond Thief on Ice

Chapter Two
The Turret Room

While other visitors bumped into one another and
began to panic, Bonnie and Grampa Banks headed
towards the upper floor, moving in the
direction the dreadful scream had
come from. Bonnie could not
help imagining the glassy eyes of
Hornville's Monsters watching her
as she creaked and squeaked her
way up the museum's old staircase.
She paused for a moment at the top
of the stairs, while Bonbon's mind
whirred to life inside her head.

Grampa Banks puffed his way up the stairs behind her, taking careful steps in his immaculate crêpe-soled shoes. In the words of Bonnie's mum, Grampa Banks was "always well turned out". He had worked as an ice-cream vendor for forty years, and never once got a blob of tutti-frutti on his outfit. To this day, he still put on a cravat before taking out the bins.

The upper floor was even darker than the main hall. Unidentifiable winged creatures hung down from the ceiling and swung gently above Bonnie's head. There was no way of knowing where exactly the scream had come from, but Bonnie could hear a **BANG, BANG, BANG, CRUNCH!** coming from near by.

"Did you hear that, Bonbon old man?" asked Grampa Banks, slightly out of breath and loosening his cravat.

"I was hearing it most clearly, Banks."

Grampa Banks always referred to Montgomery Bonbon

as "old man" or "old chap" or sometimes "old bean" – never, ever "Bonnie". Montgomery Bonbon usually referred to Grampa Banks simply as "Banks" – never, ever "Grampa". When Bonbon was not on a case, Grampa Banks was the boss. He was in charge of driving places and looking after the lemon sherbets. But when Bonbon was on a case, Bonnie was the boss; Banks was her assistant.

"Foul play, d'you reckon?" asked Grampa Banks.

"It is certainly sounding like it, *mein ami*," replied Bonnie in Montgomery Bonbon's unidentifiable foreign accent. She had learned – from wobbly old Sunday afternoon movies with Grampa Banks – that the best detectives were always from Somewhere Else.

Bonnie led the way towards the commotion, until they came to a door. It was barely illuminated by a debris-covered skylight, but she could just make out the words *Turret Room*. The splintered frame around the door told Bonnie that the **CRUNCH!** she had just heard had been the sound of someone breaking it open. Three panicked voices were whispering inside.

"Don't shine that in our faces!"

"He's dead!"

"It's gone!"

Bonnie gave a gentle push, and the crooked door swung open on groaning hinges. She already knew what she would find on the inside: a crime scene. Her eyes darted around the room in front of her, scanning for clues.

The turret room was a small, eight-sided chamber with a single yellowish window that let in very little light. The dark wood panelling on the walls made the space feel even more enclosed. On a high shelf, under a snowdrift of dust, crouched some kind of enormous rodent with huge leathery ears and tusks – another one of Hornville's creations.

In the exact centre of the chamber stood a solid marble pedestal, topped by a square glass case. The case, Bonnie noticed, was empty. Completely empty. A detective does not miss that sort of thing.

Bonnie could make out three members of museum staff, frozen in a state of panic. The first was a frizzy-haired woman wearing a tan-coloured gilet. There was nothing particularly

unusual about that, except for the fact that green plants seemed to be sprouting from her pockets. She was staring, open-mouthed, at the empty glass case.

The second member of staff was a woman with a rainbow-coloured waistcoat and a big round name badge. Bonnie deduced that she was one of the museum's guides.

The third member of staff was an old man who reminded Bonnie of a melted candle. He looked ever so pale and droopy in his shabby brown suit. He was the one holding the torch. And the blueish torch beam pointed towards a

fourth person: a barrel-chested youngish man dressed in a security guard uniform. The man was lying on the floor, which is normally unacceptable behaviour at work.

It was forgivable on this occasion, however, because the man was dead.

"Everybody to stay precisely where you are being!" shouted Bonnie, remembering to wiggle her moustache in a way that implied authority. The torch beam swung around, dazzling her. She wiggled the moustache again, in case anyone had missed it the first time.

"Who are you?" asked the woman in the rainbow waistcoat, with an American accent.

Bonnie waited for Grampa Banks to do his thing. And waited.

And waited.

She nudged him in the ribs.

"Oh, right!" he blustered. "Well now, this is the great detective Montgomery Bonbon."

"Montgomery ... Bonbon?" repeated the man who looked like a melted candle. A long pause followed, and Bonnie thought she could almost feel her moustache starting to come loose. "Thank goodness you're here, Detective. There's been a murder, you see."

"And a theft!" wailed the woman whose pockets were full of plants.

"One moment, please!" demanded Bonnie.

The plant woman bit her lip and began nervously uprooting a pocketful of peonies.

Montgomery Bonbon took very a deliberate step into the room and walked in a perfect circle around the marble pedestal.

Bonnie began her investigation in exactly the same way she explored museums. While Grampa Banks got out his old-fashioned camera and meticulously photographed everything in the room, Bonnie let instinct guide her from clue to clue.

Click, FLASH, *grrr* went Grampa Banks's camera as it snapped an image of the empty display case and whirred on to the next piece of film. Bonnie imagined the museum's foundations shivering at the prospect of the forbidden flash photography. But that was what detective work was all about: shining light into dark places.

Click, FLASH, *grrr*...

According to his name tag, the dead man was Oliver Munday. His security guard uniform looked new – almost brand new. So, thought Bonnie, he hadn't been working here long. It was spotless but for a coating of dust on his right cuff. Bonnie supposed it would be hard to spend time in the Hornville Museum without getting a little dusty, but she made a note of it all the same. A detective could not afford to overlook tiny details.

Moving closer, her eyes were drawn to what appeared to be a scarlet feather, sticking out of Oliver Munday's neck. Some kind of dart? she asked herself. Poison?

Bonnie lived for solving mysteries. She loved finding clues and she particularly liked telling adults what to do. But she did not enjoy finding dead bodies. And it seemed a special shame to find one with a face that looked as kind as Oliver Munday's.

Click, FLASH, grrr...

Bonnie spun round on her heel to face the three living museum employees. She studied them one by one.

Nearest was the old gentleman in the brown suit. According to his name tag, he was Anton Price, the museum restorer. There was something about his out-of-date clothes and his round spectacles that made him seem like he *belonged* in the museum. He was the kind of man people would describe as "thinning on top", if they had somehow forgotten the word bald.

Anton Price shuffled backwards and sat down heavily – knees cracking like breadsticks – in one of those deliciously comfortable-looking antique chairs that museum visitors are never allowed to sit in. Bonnie could feel Grampa Banks staring at him enviously.

Click, FLASH, grrr...

On the other side of the turret room, the tour guide in the rainbow waistcoat stood with her back to the window. Bonnie moved close enough to see that her name badge read, *Rashida Zaki*. Rashida looked like she was carrying out an investigation of her own. She examined the marble pedestal and then squinted up at the ceiling, as if she expected to find the killer hanging from the rafters like a bat.

When she spoke, something about Rashida's American accent seemed familiar to Bonnie. Bonnie had noticed that British people tended to be impressed by Americans, for no particular reason.

They were also impressed by tall people and people who owned a treehouse. A tall American with their own treehouse could get away with murder. But, Bonnie wondered, could Rashida Zaki?

Click, FLASH, grrr...

The third museum employee was standing next to the empty glass dome, making mulch out of the greenery in her pockets. She turned out to be Harriet Spruce, manager of the museum. Bonnie could not tell if Harriet's bottom lip was wobbling, or if Harriet was wobbling and her bottom lip was staying still. Either way, she seemed very upset.

"We couldn't get in..." Harriet was mumbling. "The door was locked."

"Let us start with you, Fräulein Spruce." Bonnie gave Harriet a tight, scrunched-up smile calculated to reassure the innocent ... and terrify the guilty. "From the very beginning, please tell to Bonbon *precisely* what happened."

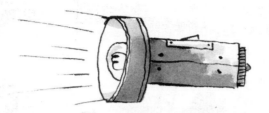

Chapter Three
The Widdlington Eagle

"Where were you when the lights, they went *poomf*?" asked Bonnie.

All eyes in the turret room were on Harriet. Apart from Oliver Munday's, of course.

"I was in the… Well, all three of us were on a tea break in the staffroom. There was a power cut, and then we heard that terrible scream! You heard it as well, Mr…?"

"*Monsieur* Bonbon," corrected Bonnie. "*Ja*, I was hearing the scream most terrible." She looked at poor Oliver Munday stretched out on the floor and had to suppress a shudder.

"I'm sorry; I'm just so…" Harriet waved her hands apologetically, sending fragments of green leaves fluttering all over the crime scene. She could only manage splutters and sobs.

Anton Price continued the story. "I picked up the torch from the emergency kit." Once again, the old man pointed the beam towards Bonnie, giving her a big green splodge in the middle of her vision. "And we all hurried here to the turret room. But the door was locked, you see. *From the inside*, you see."

Locked. From. The. Inside. The four words every detective hoped to hear. Bonnie was close enough to the door to see that Anton was telling the truth. The wood of the door frame was splintered, and she could see a rust-coloured key still in the lock on the inside. Grampa Banks snapped a picture of it.

Click, FLASH, *grrr*…

"I broke down the door." Rashida jumped in, talking excitedly. "That's when we found him." She gestured towards Oliver's body. "And we realized it was gone."

"It?" asked Bonnie. "What exactly is being gone?"

30

Three faces stared at Bonnie in astonishment.

"W-w-why, the Widdlington Eagle, of course!" said Harriet.

Bonnie's confusion must have shown on Montgomery Bonbon's face, because Grampa Banks pulled the Hornville Museum brochure out of his back pocket and thrust it under her moustache. Bonnie had been expecting to see another one of Hornville's Monsters: something with hippo legs and feathers, perhaps. But the picture in the brochure showed a beautifully carved stone eagle, looking to its right as if to say, "This is my good side."

WIDDLINGTON EAGLE

ABELARD HORNVILLE

The statuette was sitting inside the glass case that now stood empty in the centre of the room. According to the description, the Widdlington Eagle was *a fabulously rare find from Roman Britain, unearthed by Abelard Hornville (1897–1985) himself in 1930. It is now on loan for the first time from the New Jersey Museum for Neat Old Stuff.*

Bonnie looked up. "This Widdly Eagle … she is being most valuable, *ja*?"

Three heads nodded vigorously.

"*Bon*," replied Bonnie.

Bon was what Montgomery Bonbon said whenever Bonnie needed a moment to think. She folded up the brochure and steepled her fingers under her nose. She had never really understood why adults thought certain things were worth such a lot of money, but her opinion of the Widdlington Eagle was not what mattered. It looked like someone had been prepared to kill for it.

"And the eagle, she was gone when you entered the room, *non*?"

Three heads nodded once again.

Hmm, thought Bonnie as she scanned the room. Since the door was locked from the inside, the only way in or out would be … through the turret room's single window. The window was a narrow oblong, with strips of lead making diamonds of the uneven, yellowish glass. The latch was open, and the window hung very slightly ajar. Being careful not to touch the latch, Bonnie levered the window wide open.

She blinked in the daylight. The sounds of Business as Usual drifted on the breeze. The rest of the town did not know that time had stopped in the Hornville Museum. Widdlington did not yet know that something was afoot.

Bonnie looked out at the roof of the museum: a higgledy-piggledy jumble of sloping tiles and irregular chimney stacks. A section of flat roof created a narrow walkway, stretching away from the window towards the top of a crooked-looking fire escape.

Click, FLASH, grrr…

Could a shadowy assassin have made their way up that fire escape, Bonnie asked herself, then crunched across the gravel on the roof, creaked open the window and…

Just as she was about to finish that thought, Rashida appeared at Bonnie's shoulder.

"The fire escape! Of course!" she exclaimed, barrelling past Bonnie and almost knocking Grampa Banks's camera out of his hands. Before Montgomery Bonbon could shout, "*Arrêtez!*" Rashida had clambered out of the window.

"*Non!* We must disturb nothing about the crime scene!" Bonnie shouted, but she knew she was wasting her breath. Rashida was already skidding across the gravel.

"He must've got out this way!" Rashida yelled back as she began climbing down the fire escape ladder. "You wanna catch the thief, right?"

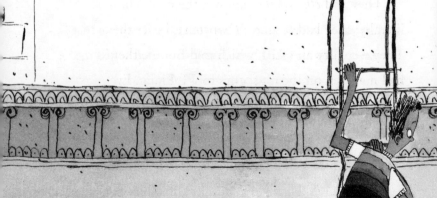

Bonnie *did* wanna catch the thief, right. And to do that, she needed clues. Her hopes of finding the outline of an assassin's footprint in the gravel outside the window had been dashed the instant the museum guide blundered out there. Now there was nothing but grey gravel, dry dust and...

What was *that*?

Two tiny yellowish specks were lying on the flat roof, just below the window. As Bonnie carefully pinched them out of the gravel, she saw that they were torn and raggedy scraps of paper, each no larger than her fingernail. In faded blue ink, one of them read *61* and the other *1E*.

They had *clue* written all over them. (Well, not literally; they had *61* and *1E* written all over them.) They were dry and stiff, which told Bonnie they had not been on the museum's roof for long. Even in summer, Widdlington's wind and rain would have obliterated them overnight. But what on earth could they mean?

Click, FLASH, grrr...

"What do you reckon?" asked Grampa Banks under his breath. "Some kind of code? A map reference?"

Bonnie was not sure, so she just murmured, "*Bon.*" Fortunately, that seemed to satisfy Grampa Banks.

In the room behind her, Anton Price cleared his throat nervously. "Detective, do you think… That is to say…"

Bonnie pocketed the scraps of paper carefully and swung round, freezing Harriet and Anton to the spot with her expression. The expression in question involved opening one eye very wide, and narrowing the other like a letter box. Bonnie had practised this in front of the mirror with the express purpose of freezing people to the spot. This was the first time she had used it, and she was pleased with the result.

"Let me remind you, good people, that this is being a crime scene. Nobody touches anything and nobody else *leaves* without the permission of Bonbon," she said. A moustache wiggle was unnecessary. "Monsieur Price, pray continue."

Anton Price awkwardly shuffled the cuffs of his corduroy jacket. "You see, I … I rather think we ought to call the police."

"No need, sunshine," came a familiar voice from the corridor, followed by an unmistakable *clomp, clomp, clomp* which Bonnie had come to associate with impending disaster. It was the sound of Inspector Prashanti Sands of Widdlington Constabulary. Inspector Sands always wore boots that were two sizes too large. Bonnie suspected she did this so she could wriggle her toes gleefully whenever she said things like, "No need, sunshine," "Just doing my job, sir," and "You're nicked!"

Bonnie took a deep breath and tried to look on the bright side. In a way, it was good news that Inspector Sands had arrived. Most senior officers at Widdlington Police Station *absolutely despised* Montgomery Bonbon.

Inspector Sands merely loathed him.

Chapter Four
Inspector Sands

Inspector Sands had not looked surprised upon finding Montgomery Bonbon at the crime scene. She had not looked particularly *pleased*, but definitely not surprised.

It is an unbreakable law of the universe that brilliant detectives are always present when mysterious murders are committed. A decent detective can hardly eat breakfast without finding a corpse in their choccy rice flakes. Inspector Sands did not have this problem. In Bonnie's opinion, this was a dead giveaway that Sands was not a proper detective. That, and her inability to solve tricky crimes without the help of Montgomery Bonbon.

"No CCTV?" repeated the inspector, agog. "Are you telling me that you've got a … what *is* that? A giant rat?"

"It's a squirrelephant," replied Harriet quietly.

"Are you telling me you've got a flippin' massive *squirreffelant*, but you don't have any security cameras?" Inspector Sands blinked in amazement. Bonnie had noticed that she always got irritated when it looked like she was going to have to actually *investigate* a crime.

"Mr Hornville – he's the museum's owner – he always seems to know what's happening anyway. So we've never needed security cameras. And, you know, visitors really do like the squirrelephant…" Harriet trailed off, staring down at her plants.

By now, power had been restored to the museum and the lights were back on. The Hornville's caretaker, a woman in tatty overalls, had popped in and said something to Inspector Sands about the fuse box, muttering so quietly that Bonnie had barely managed to catch a word. Sands had dismissed her imperiously and the caretaker was now pacing around outside the turret room looking put out.

Meanwhile, Rashida had returned, dejected and empty-handed. As far as Bonnie could tell, she had not succeeded in recovering the Widdlington Eagle.

"Get that to the crime lab, ASAP as possible," ordered Sands as a police constable slid the red feathered dart into an evidence bag.

The inspector was stomping all over the crime scene, asking the same questions Bonnie had but in a much louder voice. Her hair was pulled back into a severe-looking bun with a fountain pen sticking out of it. Occasionally she slid the pen out and poked something with it: furniture, people, Grampa Banks. The pen-poking must have worked, because she straightened up after a long minute of prodding the empty glass case and announced, "Right, that's that. Everybody out."

Nobody moved. Harriet, Anton and Rashida glanced towards Bonnie, seeking permission to leave. Montgomery Bonbon could not stop his moustache from twitching a little with pride.

"Oh. Forgot about you, Bonbon," said the inspector brusquely. "You're not planning on sticking your beak into police business again, are you? Seems fairly clear cut to me."

"It does, Inspecteur?" asked Bonnie, not daring to allow her moustache the slightest wobble.

"Obvious, innit? When the lights went out, whatsisname on the floor there locked the door to protect the thingumabob in the glass case. Then what happens? He hears some noises over by the window. The window what can only be opened from this side, mark you."

The inspector gave Bonnie a look that said, "Didn't reckon I'd spot that, did you?"

Bonnie resisted the temptation to roll her eyes.

"So, matey boy here opens the window to see what all the commotion is and – *THWUUM!* – blow dart to the neck."

Inspector Sands was acting out her theory with what Bonnie thought was far too much arm-flailing.

"He goes down – *BAM!* – and the killer hops in. They nab the doodad on the pedestal, hop back out and scarper. Based on Miss…"

"Zaki," supplied Rashida.

"Based on Miss Zaki sweating cobs over there – no offence – we're looking for someone who can scale a building and still has enough puff left to use a blowpipe." Bonnie noticed a glint in the inspector's eyes. "The Blowpipe Killer. Hey, that's got a ring to it!"

Bonnie, grudgingly, had to agree. It did have a ring to it.

"My girls, and young Simon, bless him, will be all over this in no time. These cat-burglar types, they always slip up. They're too ... what's the word? Too..."

"Arrogant?" said Bonnie. "Pompous? Proud? Big-headed?"

"All right, all right," said Inspector Sands. "I didn't ask for the flippin'—"

"Thesaurus?" Bonnie suggested.

"Just like you to bring dinosaurs into this, Bonbon," said Inspector Sands, and Grampa Banks turned a chuckle into a cough. "This ain't about thesauruses or bloomin' squirreffelants. It's about regular police business, not that you'd know anything about that. Here, what's the matter with him?"

Grampa Banks, eyes watering, still stifling a laugh, was now making a noise like a wildcat stuck in a bread bin.

"All right, I've had enough. We've got police work to do."

Inspector Sands began herding the museum staff out of the turret room, making space for junior police officers to scuttle around the scene, trying to look busy. Now was the moment for Bonnie to tell Widdlington's finest about the clue she had discovered outside the window…

"What're you waiting for, Bonbon? Gerrout of it!"

Maybe not, she thought as she followed Grampa Banks away from the crime scene.

The upper floor of the Hornville Museum looked slightly less sinister now that the lights were back on. Standing on tiptoes to look over the balustrade, Bonnie could see a huddle of worried museum visitors in the centre of the main hall, with police uniforms dotted around the room.

Click, FLASH, grrr…

"That'd better not be a picture of me, matey boy," Inspector Sands warned Grampa Banks.

A man strode in through the Hornville Museum's front entrance. Bonnie expected one of the coppers to try to stop him, but they did not. Perhaps this was because the man walked like he owned the place. Perhaps it was because he was *dressed* like he owned the place. Perhaps it was because he owned the place.

"Mr Hornville! It's a disaster!" wailed Harriet, hurrying down the staircase, closely followed by Inspector Sands.

"He must be the boss," said Grampa Banks, pointing Bonnie towards a life-size portrait of the tall, stern-looking man that was hanging at the top of the staircase. Bonnie shuffled closer. According to the brass plaque, he was Herman Hornville, the grandson of the museum's founder. He wore shoes that clacked as he crossed the parquet floor, and one of those small triangular beards that make people worry the wearer is about to do a card trick.

"We came as soon as we got your call, Mr Hornville," said Inspector Sands in a syrupy voice that Bonnie had never heard her use before. She began explaining the crime to him, while Harriet and Rashida watched, wide-eyed. Even Anton Price seemed to be listening carefully while he *squeak-squeak-squawked* an old cleaning trolley around the displays, carefully brushing the bones of a manatee-rex.

With all the focus on the inspector, no one apart from Bonnie seemed to notice the girl who slipped into the museum behind Herman Hornville. There was something spooky about her old-fashioned clothes and the way she drifted through the visitors without drawing anyone's attention. She was around Bonnie's age, or perhaps a little older. Bonnie was almost ready to believe she was a ghost, until she took hold of Herman Hornville's hand.

His daughter? Bonnie wondered. I'd love to know where those two were during the murder…

The inspector's tale of blow darts and daring rooftop escapes was coming to a close.

"So you see, Mr Hornville, sir," she concluded, "it's all very simple. Right now, we just need everybody out."

The people huddling around Herman Hornville looked frightened and confused; Bonnie wanted them to know that Montgomery Bonbon was on the case. She hurried down the stairs.

"Please to be excusing me, Inspecteur…" began Bonnie, choosing her words carefully. She had to be tactful. Her investigation would be very difficult if she got on the wrong side of Prashanti Sands. But she couldn't let an important fact go unnoticed.

"It is a small coincidence that the lights went out *just* before the murder, *ja*?"

"I was about to say that, actually," Inspector Sands lied. "It is a bit of a coincidence that the whatsits went out just before the oojamaflip."

"And the killer was knowing exactly which

48

window to go for. So perhaps they—"

"Perhaps they had help from someone inside the museum. Yes. That's what I was about to say to Mr Hornville." Inspector Sands took a deep breath and yelled, "SIMON!"

"Ma'am?" said the gawkish police constable standing just behind her.

"Where have you been hiding, Simon? When you've finished taking statements, I want *everybody* searched. You never know, we may have an inside man. Or person."

"Yes, ma'am."

A murmur rippled through the room. A search? An inside man? Or person?

"We won't need to search *you*, Mr Hornville," said Sands in what she probably thought was a whisper. "Just the plebs."

"Oh, no, you must. I insist," replied Herman Hornville. The man's voice reminded Bonnie of an old oak tree creaking. His face was as still as the creatures in the glass cases around him. Was he sad to have lost the priceless Widdlington Eagle? Angry? Relieved?

Bonnie could not tell.

Click, FLASH, *grrr*...

Grampa Banks had gone a step too far, taking a picture of Herman Hornville.

"All right, Bonbon, that's it. I've had enough of you and Mr Snap Happy here."

"Just one more thing!" said Bonnie quickly as a police constable came up from behind and clamped a hand onto Montgomery Bonbon's shoulder. "Perhaps you should be posting an officer to guard the museum? *Non?*"

"*Non!* I mean, no! No, I couldn't do that. Not to our Simon. Not on poker night," said Inspector Sands. "Anyway, it's hardly necessary. A criminal *never* returns to the scene of the crime. Thought you'd have heard that one, Bonbon." She gave Herman Hornville a look. "Seems like the amateurs don't know everything, eh?"

Bonnie hoped the inspector could not hear her gritting her teeth.

"Now, I mean it this time," continued Inspector Sands. **"EVERYBODY OUT!"**

Chapter Five
Dead End

Bonnie's home did not look very much like the
residence of the world's finest detective. The
entrance to 321 Dead End was not flanked by stone
bloodhounds, and the hallway did not echo with the
imposing *tick-tock* of a grandfather clock. Whoever
built the house had forgotten to put in a secret attic.
Or a secret basement. Or a bookcase that spun round
to reveal a secret attic-basement. Bonnie had checked.
Many times.

"So what's the plan, eh, love?" asked Grampa Banks
as they approached their house. "Hunt for clues? Grill
the suspects one by one? Lay a trap for the killer?"

"Let us see where the case leads us, *mein ami*," replied Bonnie with a smile. Her assistant always wanted to know what the plan was. He wanted to solve cases the way he explored museums: step by step. But murders were not like museums. They were not supposed to make sense. They did not even have gift shops.

Grampa Banks squeaked the front door open, and Bonnie heard a full-bodied "Hallooo!" that could only have come from her mum. Liz Montgomery was a boisterous woman, bubbling with love for Bonnie, and with a tendency to sing loudly and without warning. Her only real drawback, as a mum, was that she was not interested in murder. Hardly at all. For that reason, Bonnie's mum had never met Montgomery Bonbon. And as far as Bonnie was concerned, she never would.

Bonnie accepted a wet kiss from Liz, cunningly dodged a lengthy hug and thudded up the stairs. She could hardly explain to her mother that she had found two mysterious scraps of paper at a crime scene, and she needed to add them to her clue collection.

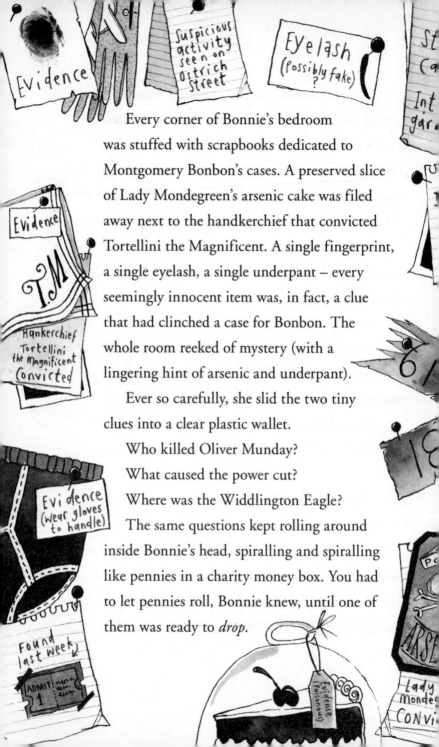

Every corner of Bonnie's bedroom was stuffed with scrapbooks dedicated to Montgomery Bonbon's cases. A preserved slice of Lady Mondegreen's arsenic cake was filed away next to the handkerchief that convicted Tortellini the Magnificent. A single fingerprint, a single eyelash, a single underpant – every seemingly innocent item was, in fact, a clue that had clinched a case for Bonbon. The whole room reeked of mystery (with a lingering hint of arsenic and underpant).

Ever so carefully, she slid the two tiny clues into a clear plastic wallet.

Who killed Oliver Munday?

What caused the power cut?

Where was the Widdlington Eagle?

The same questions kept rolling around inside Bonnie's head, spiralling and spiralling like pennies in a charity money box. You had to let pennies roll, Bonnie knew, until one of them was ready to *drop*.

An hour later, Bonnie and Liz were seated around a small table in the middle of the kitchen, while Grampa Banks dished up three bowls of rice and beans. Bonnie could not speak freely about the case in front of her mum, but that was not going to stop her talking about it.

"…and Montgomery Bonbon was there, and he was brilliant! And then Inspector Sands blundered in; she's such a jellybrain, Mum!"

"That's a very unkind thing to say about a very important grown-up, Bonnie."

"But it's true! She's a massive jellybrain. Tell her, Grampa!"

Bonnie stared at Grampa Banks expectantly. He looked at Liz. He looked at Bonnie. He looked back at Liz.

"She is a *bit* of a jellybrain."

"See!" Bonnie threw her hands in the air triumphantly, sending the red kidney bean on her fork flying off on a journey into the unknown. It was the Neil Armstrong of beans, travelling where no bean had gone before.

Grampa Banks nudged Bonnie gently. "Reckon your mum has heard enough about Monsieur Bonbon for one evening, hmm?"

"I suppose. Maybe we could listen to *History's Mysterious Mysteries*?" suggested Bonnie.

"Maybe we've had enough murder and enough mystery for one evening," said Bonnie's mum firmly. "Would anyone like to hear about my day?"

Bonnie slumped down in her chair. "I would love to hear about your day," she murmured.

Liz Montgomery worked as a lab assistant in the science wing of Widdlington Sports College and Mule Sanctuary, but her passion was for all things spiritual. Sometimes that meant smelly candles, sometimes it meant dangly crystals, but usually it involved giving quite a lot of money to someone called Guru Jonathan Jonathan. This week, Bonnie's mum was talking about something called "the third eye".

"Well, according to Guru Jonathan Jonathan," she began, "we all have a third eye, and it lets you see beyond this reality into the astral plane."

"I thought you were supposed to be a scientist,

Mum," protested Bonnie, who was sure Liz had never even *flown* on an astral plane.

"There's one thing that every good scientist needs," said Bonnie's mum, tapping her forehead, "and that is a bit of imagination."

Bonnie sighed inwardly, but tried her best to look interested. While her mum talked, she began to replay the day's events in her mind.

Three members of museum staff had found a body: Harriet Spruce, Anton Price and Rashida Zaki. They were together when they heard Oliver Munday scream, so they all had an alibi for his murder. Or, thought Bonnie, all three of them could be lying.

They broke down the door to the turret room, and immediately saw that the Widdlington Eagle had been stolen by someone who had escaped onto the roof and down the fire escape. But how did the killer know when the lights were going to go out? Were they working with someone inside the museum?

Then there was the austere Herman Hornville and his ghostly daughter. Where had they been when the poisoner attacked? They only appeared on the scene after the body had been discovered. Either of them, Bonnie mused, could have poisoned Oliver and stolen the Widdlington Eagle.

"Interesting…" she muttered.

"That's exactly what I said to Guru Jonathan Jonathan!" said her mum.

Bonnie knew that the human brain was good at making connections. A little too good, sometimes. This is why you can see scary faces in wallpaper patterns and gnarly old trees. A detective had to be able to tell the difference between appearances and reality, and that was what Bonnie tried to do now.

While she shifted beans around on her plate, she went over the facts one more time. Three witnesses broke down the door and saw that the Widdlington Eagle had been stolen by someone who had escaped through the window…

But what did they *really* see? A dead body, an empty glass case and an open window. Nobody actually *saw* the killer clamber down the fire escape with the priceless exhibit. Maybe someone wanted them to *think* the eagle had been taken. An old building like the Hornville had to be full of potential hiding places.

Of course! Bonnie could almost hear the sound of a penny dropping. The killer could have hidden the eagle away somewhere, for the inside man (or person) to collect later. She should never have let Inspector Sands shoo Montgomery Bonbon from the crime scene.

"We must act fast," she said to herself. If she had been wearing a moustache, she would have wiggled it.

"Do you really think so?" asked her mum, with a note of surprise.

Bonnie realized that she had blundered into the middle of a conversation she had not been listening to. Her only option was to commit.

"Um … yes. Absolutely. One hundred per cent." Bonnie hoped she was agreeing to getting a puppy.

Liz beamed. "I didn't think you'd be so enthusiastic."

Bonnie watched a puppy disappear before her third eye. "Oh, I'm very enthusiastic! Wait a moment – is that the time? I'd better get off to bed. *Phew-ee!*"

Bonnie faked a yawn, stretching her arms over her head and sending a second red kidney bean flying off the end of her fork. It was the Buzz Aldrin of beans.

"What. A. Day!" she continued. "I'll sleep tonight! Love you, Mum. Good night!" In one movement, she slid down from her chair and out of the kitchen door, murmuring, "GrampacanItalktoyouforaminute?" as she disappeared.

Grampa Banks shrugged at Bonnie's mum before getting up and following. Liz Montgomery was left sitting, as she often was after a conversation with her daughter, scratching her head. Bonnie was halfway down the corridor when she heard her mother's bemused voice from the kitchen.

"Why are there *beans* in my hair?!"

"Good news, Banks," announced Bonnie as soon as they were alone. "I think the Widdlington Eagle could still be in the turret room at the museum."

"It's *Grampa* when we're at home… But hold on, you mean it *wasn't* stolen?"

"No, it was definitely stolen. Just not completely. Maybe. If I'm right, then the killer's accomplice could be on their way to collect it right now. We might be able to catch them!"

"And who is the killer's accomplice?" asked Grampa Banks.

"The one who turned out the lights."

"Right… Who's that, then?"

"That's what we're going to find out – on a *stake-out*," said Bonnie gleefully.

"Oh, no, no, no." Grampa Banks folded his arms.

"You know how your mother feels about you being out after dark."

"Come on!" Bonnie pleaded. "It's an emergency."

Grampa Banks knitted his brows.

"You wanted to know what the plan was? Well, this is the plan! A stake-out."

Grampa Banks tried to fold his legs.

"Can we put it on the Tab? Please?" she asked, trying to look as endearing as possible. The Tab was a record of every family rule, local ordinance and natural law that Bonnie had broken while pursuing a case as Montgomery Bonbon. At the last count, she was due to be grounded for roughly nine years.

Grampa Banks crumpled. Reluctantly he pulled a small notebook from his back pocket. He licked the end of a stubby yellow pencil and wrote: *Sneaking out after teatime* underneath *Impersonating a ventriloquist.*

By the time Grampa Banks looked up, Bonnie was already wearing her false moustache.

He sighed, defeated. "I'll start Bessie."

THE TAB (CONT'D)

- POSSESSION OF AN OFFENSIVE CHEESE
- SPEAKING TO THE DRIVER WHILE THE BUS IS MOVING
- ATTEMPTED SHRUBBERY
- BRINGING SEVEN ITEMS TO THE 'FIVE ITEMS OR LESS' CHECKOUT
- TRESPASSING
- UNAUTHORIZED SURVEILLANCE OF A VICAR
- CLIMBING THROUGH THE KITCHEN HATCH TO GRAMPA BANK'S ROOM
- BADGERING A WITNESS
- BADGERING A BADGER
- IMPERSONATING A VENTRILOQUIST
- SNEAKING OUT AFTER TEATIME

Chapter Six
The Stake-out

It was midnight, and Widdlington's streets were quiet. No cars were rumbling down Museum Street; no coaches were bound for Widdle Cove. In the gentle rain, wet pavements reflected the traffic lights changing silently from red to green, as if rehearsing for a busy day tomorrow.

The façade of the Hornville Museum was adorned with stone carvings of naked people. As far as Bonnie could tell, they seemed to be fighting over a bunch of grapes. For some reason, it was fine to go around with no clothes on as long as you were made of stone. Bonnie did not understand this, but she knew it to

be true. A large-scale grape fight had recently broken out at Widdlington's Fruit Market. When the town crier had taken his shirt off, the organizers had called the cops. Inspector Sands had arrested the grapes.

An old ice-cream van named Bessie was parked across the street from the museum. After he had retired, Grampa Banks had painted Bessie the most boring shade of grey he could find – it was called Sunday Drizzle. His plan had been to stop the local kids chasing Bessie down the street. Now she looked exactly like every other grey van.

Apart from the enormous grey ice-cream cone sticking out of her roof.

Bonnie had asked Grampa Banks to park where they could see not only the Hornville's main entrance, but also the side door, accessible through an alleyway called Goose Chase. She was relieved to see that both doors were still criss-crossed with blue-and-white police tape screaming:

Bonnie was not sure whether this was a warning, or Widdlington Constabulary's motto. However, the presence of the tape meant that no one had passed through those doors since the cops had cleared out.

Bonnie had forgotten how boring stake-outs could be. She was sitting in Bessie's passenger seat, watching and waiting for an accomplice who might never arrive. She could usually rely on Grampa Banks to help pass the time, but he was snoring like a vacuum cleaner full of soup. She had tried listening to an episode of the *History's Mysterious Mysteries* podcast, but the soothing voice of Madison Garden was not enough to stop her thoughts from hopping like popcorn in a pan.

What if she was wrong and the Widdlington Eagle was already gone? What if the accomplice was clambering up the fire escape right now? Or making off with the prize while Bonnie kicked her heels?

If the eagle was still in the turret room, she needed to find it. Before someone else did.

Grampa Banks could add *Breaking into a crime scene* to the Tab when he woke up.

Bonnie opened the passenger door as quietly as

she could and dropped down into the street. She stuck Montgomery Bonbon's sticky moustache to her upper lip and pulled on the old raincoat, then tiptoed across the empty street towards Goose Chase. All Bonnie could hear was the chatter of the rain, the distant murmur of the sea and Grampa Banks putting the Olympic snoring champion to shame. The alleyway was narrow and very dark, as though the light from the street lamps was afraid of straying too far from the pavement.

She stepped over a discarded edition of Widdlington's local newspaper, *The Widdler*, which was turning into papier mâché on the wet paving stones. In the darkest depths of the alleyway she discovered the museum's wrought-iron fire escape, stretching up two storeys to the roof. Bonnie had been picturing a reassuringly solid staircase devoted to saving lives in the event of a fire. The sinister, warped and rusting ladder in front of her looked more likely to *start* a fire – and claim the insurance.

No one had entered the museum from ground level, Bonnie could be sure about that. The doors were locked shut, the police tape untouched. The next place to check was the window to the turret room, and that meant climbing all the way up to the top of the building.

It was a *very* rickety ladder, thought Bonnie.

She could have crept back to Bessie's warm, dry passenger seat, but the faint itch of Montgomery Bonbon's moustache reminded her that there was a case to be solved. She began to climb.

The rungs of the ladder were cold and slippery, and the metal groaned as Bonnie slowly ascended. Every step she took seemed to produce a new creak or a moan – not exactly ideal for sneaking in quietly, she noted. Every now and then, a gust of wind would set the whole frame rattling, and Bonnie would close her eyes and imagine the ladder coming loose from the wall and falling backwards and...

No.

Montgomery Bonbon was no man of action, but he was certainly no coward, either. Bonnie forced herself to open her

69

eyes and focus on the rung of the ladder in front of her. Peering over her moustache, and squinting in the rain, she carried on climbing up.

Up.

Up.

Up, to the very top. And that was when she spotted it.

As her eyes drew level with the very top of the wall, Bonnie saw something almost hidden in the crack between two weathered red bricks. It was a little metal object, glittering faintly in the moonlight: a silver hairpin in the shape of a pretty little flower.

A strange thing to find at the top of a fire escape.

Tonight's investigation was going well. She had hardly risked her life at all, and she had already found another clue. It was a well-known fact that hairpins could be used to pick locks. If Bonnie were being honest with herself, she did not know exactly how hairpins could be used to pick locks. Despite all the criminals she had studied, from the Aquarium Arsonist to the Zirconium Zombie, she had never heard of anyone *actually* picking a lock using a hairpin. But every mystery book she had read and every TV show she had seen told her that it could be done.

Bonnie climbed the last few steps onto the roof, carefully secured the hairpin in her raincoat pocket and tried to catch her breath. Looking around, she saw the rooftops of Widdlington spread out below her like a jagged mountain range. The Hornville stood in the middle of the Old Town, which had been built by Victorians with more money than architectural talent. That meant Bonnie looked down on domes and spires and dormer windows so large they had their own smaller dormer windows on top. But the roof felt strangely private. She needed only to crouch and she would have vanished completely from view.

The turret room looked a great deal more imposing from the outside. Its sharp roof was silhouetted against the moon; its octagonal walls were topped with nasty little spikes designed to make pigeons – or anyone else – think twice before having a poo. Bonnie crunched cautiously across the gravel towards it, past murky-looking skylights, back along the path Rashida Zaki had followed earlier.

She walked slowly, listening carefully in case there was anyone lurking in a shadowy corner. The turret room's window was closed and locked. A strip of police tape ran across it, once again reading:

POLICE - DON'T EVEN THINK ABOUT IT

In blue marker pen someone had added:

THIS MEANS YOU, BONBON!

Bonnie had mixed feelings about the locked window. It meant no one had entered the museum since the murder, but it also meant she could not get inside to have a proper nose around the crime scene. She examined the window again – the hinges, the frame, the streaked glass... It really could not be opened from the outside.

She was just beginning to look forward to a long night playing I Spy with Grampa Banks when she saw something.

It was a light, flashing inside the turret room. The yellow glass shimmered for a split-second and then went dark. Then it flashed again. Someone was moving around inside the museum with a torch.

Bonnie had just managed to steady her breathing after climbing up the fire escape; now her heart was set racing again. Could this be the killer's accomplice, returned to make off with the Widdlington Eagle in the dead of night?

There was no way Bonnie could get inside; there was no one she could call. Bonnie huffed in frustration. If only Inspector Sands had posted a guard!

After a moment of panic, Bonnie realized that she did have one option. She drew herself up to Montgomery Bonbon's full height – which was not very high – straightened the raincoat's collar, puffed up her moustache and rapped, very politely, on the glass.

The beam of torchlight swung round and pointed straight at the window. A yellowish haze lit up the rooftop around Bonnie. She steeled herself and knocked again.

"'Allo in there!" she called in a loud voice that she hoped sounded both confident and like someone who was allowed to be on museum rooftops at night. "Please to be opening the window." She thought for a moment and added, "Most immediately!"

The light inside began to bob towards the window. Bonnie strained to make out who was holding the torch, but all she could see was dirty glass and torchlight. Then, after a brief rattling noise, the window squeaked open a crack and a voice that Bonnie did not recognize said, "Who is it?"

"It is Montgomery Bonbon," replied Bonnie. With a twinge of self-doubt she added, "The great detective!"

Possible hiding places for Eagle

loose floorboards?

check under posh chairs

Bins?

disguised as a lamp?

Fire Escape

Roof

Window

missing Eagle

door

"You better come in, I s'pose," said the voice, and the turret window swung open wide, ripping the police tape and forcing Bonnie to jump backwards. Bonnie reasoned that no thief worth their salt would invite a detective into the scene of the crime, so she took a deep breath, held it – and hopped inside.

Bonnie found herself dazzled once again by a beam of blueish torchlight. As her eyes adjusted, she let her breath out with a rush of relief. "I know you!"

The woman standing in front of her wore a pair of overalls that it would be generous to describe as blue. In fact, it was generous to describe them as overalls, because they had so many rips and patches that Bonnie could see at least one elbow and several knees. The woman's age was hard for Bonnie to judge, but her clothes looked older than some of the museum exhibits. Bonnie had seen her only that afternoon, speaking to Inspector Sands after the murder. It was the Hornville's caretaker.

Her name, Bonnie learned, was Warboys. Bonnie was not sure whether Warboys was her first name, her last name, her nickname, or simply a noise that was fun to say.

Warboys stood blocking the doorway of the turret room with an electric torch in one hand and an old plastic kettle in the other.

"What are you doing here?" asked Bonnie and Warboys at the same time, their voices harmonizing strangely.

"I live here!" continued the caretaker defiantly. "You from the police?"

Bonnie did not have much time to think, but something in Warboys's tone told her that the caretaker was not a fan of the local constabulary.

Montgomery Bonbon needed to try a gentler approach.

"*Non, mein ami.* I am not being with the police. Montgomery Bonbon, he is a private investigator."

Warboys swung her kettle back and forth a few times and then grunted, "Good."

The caretaker seemed to relax a little and so Bonnie began to relax too. She started to search the turret room, running her fingers along the wooden panelling, hunting for a loose floorboard, a sliding panel, an alcove, a hollow, a niche, a nook. Heck, Bonnie would have been happy with a cranny.

She tried to keep Warboys talking while she looked for any place where the Widdlington Eagle might be hidden.

"May I be asking … why did you not leave when the Inspecteur Sands, she commanded it?"

"She told me to go home, and I already was. So I stayed where I was. Home." Warboys paused for a moment, seemed to decide that what she had said made sense, and nodded.

"Din't like that inspector," she added. "Wasn't interested in my kettle." As if to emphasize her point,

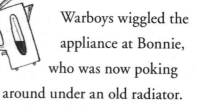

Warboys wiggled the appliance at Bonnie, who was now poking around under an old radiator. The kettle did not look particularly remarkable to Bonnie. It was one of the blandest, dullest, most ordinary kettles she had ever seen. If that kettle ever committed a crime, the kettle next door would go on the news and say, "We'd never have guessed. It seemed so normal."

Nevertheless, Bonnie decided she had to play along if she wanted to stay on Warboys's good side.

"Oh, *ja!*" she said, wriggling her fingernails into the cracks in the wainscoting, "a most interesting appliance!"

"S'not *that* interesting," sniffed Warboys. "Just went a-wandering. Very odd."

Bonnie dusted fluff off her hands and clucked her tongue in frustration. She had been all around the room twice over, knocking and tapping and scratching, and she had found nothing but dust and splinters. No secret hiding places. If the Widdlington Eagle was concealed anywhere, it was not in the turret room. Her gut had told her she would stumble across *something*. But apart from the hairpin...

She glanced sideways at Warboys. The caretaker's close-cropped hair screamed, "I cut it myself." Warboys did not look like she had a use for a dainty hairpin like the one Bonnie had found, but she might know who it belonged to. Bonnie drew it out of her pocket and let it glint in the torchlight.

"Good Warboys, please to tell me," she began, "do you recognize this?"

The caretaker stepped closer, looming over Bonnie, and squinted down at the clue. "Yep."

"Pray, continue!" said Bonnie excitedly.

"It's a hairpin," replied Warboys with satisfaction. "For pinning hair," she added, when she saw Bonnie's expression.

"Ahem." Bonnie tried again. "Do you know who this particular hairpin is belonging to?"

Warboys shrugged a shrug that seemed to start in her arms and ripple through her whole body. "Prob'ly herself."

"Herself? Who is *herself*?"

"Miss Spruce. Absolutely mad for flowers." Warboys leaned down towards Bonnie until their noses almost touched, and whispered breathily, "I reckon summat ain't right about that one."

Bonnie blinked. Somehow Warboys had spotted a connection that she had missed. So, the hairpin *might* belong to—

CREAK.

A sound made Bonnie forget all about flowers and hairpins and even caretakers' noses. The hush of the night was pierced by a long and rusty creaking noise that quivered through the museum like a chill up your spine. It could have been the groan of a dinosaur who had come back to life to find itself with the legs of a wombat. But Bonnie knew that the sound meant exactly one thing: *someone* was breaking in.

"Now, who could that be?" said Warboys with alarm. "'S'meant to be locked. Checked both entrances myself!"

Bonnie pressed her finger to her lips and gestured for Warboys to lead the way to the source of the noise. They hurried out of the turret room and tiptoed down the grand staircase. The main entrance still appeared to be locked tight.

"Must be the side door," rumbled Warboys, as they began weaving through a warren of smaller rooms. When it came to stealth, Warboys was not exactly gifted. It would have been quieter if Bonnie had been dragging a mattress full of maracas with her. But if she was about to catch the killer's accomplice red-handed, she needed a witness.

The pair stopped in front of a door with a hand-painted sign that read: **Storeroom. STAFF ONLY.** Bonnie pressed her ear against the wood, and her moustache shivered as she heard the sound of movement on the other side.

"Is it … them?" asked Warboys in what she presumably thought was a whisper. "The one who killed Oliver?"

Bonnie did not know the answer to that question,

so she did not answer. Instead she switched off Warboys's torch and then, ever so gently, began to push open the storeroom door. "You. Stay. Here," Bonnie mouthed, "And. *Watch*."

Warboys nodded. Then, for some reason, saluted.

The main galleries of the Hornville Museum were far from orderly. You could find a rare mandolin next to a fossilized ammonite next to a grizzly Beardale terrier. The storeroom was even worse: seemingly endless towers of crates and chests, vanishing into the gloom.

Bonnie held her breath and moved softly into the windowless maze where the Hornville's dusty and forgotten treasures slept. She tried not to think about the exotic creepy-crawlies that probably lived in a place like this, dangling from the nose of a broken statue or spinning a web in the mouth of a priceless vase – hairy and tickly and impossible to spot until they...

Bonnie shook her head, moustache wobbling reassuringly. She needed to concentrate. There was something much bigger and much nastier than a spider lurking in the dark tonight.

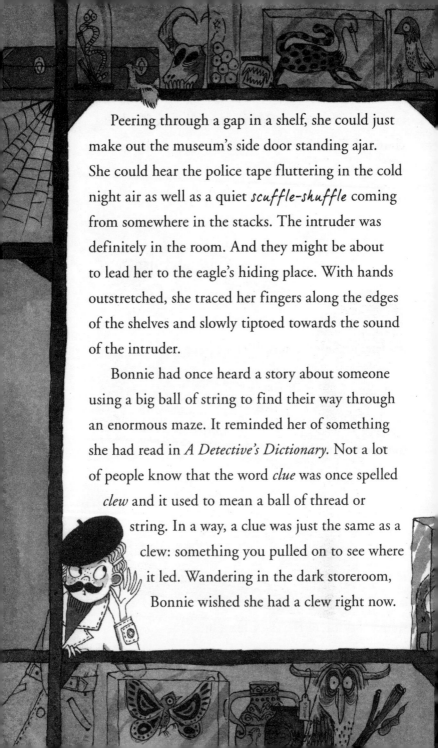

Peering through a gap in a shelf, she could just make out the museum's side door standing ajar. She could hear the police tape fluttering in the cold night air as well as a quiet *scuffle-shuffle* coming from somewhere in the stacks. The intruder was definitely in the room. And they might be about to lead her to the eagle's hiding place. With hands outstretched, she traced her fingers along the edges of the shelves and slowly tiptoed towards the sound of the intruder.

Bonnie had once heard a story about someone using a big ball of string to find their way through an enormous maze. It reminded her of something she had read in *A Detective's Dictionary*. Not a lot of people know that the word *clue* was once spelled *clew* and it used to mean a ball of thread or string. In a way, a clue was just the same as a clew: something you pulled on to see where it led. Wandering in the dark storeroom, Bonnie wished she had a clew right now.

Suddenly she stopped dead.

The intruder's distinctive *scuffle-shuffle* had changed. Bonnie realized that she was no longer moving towards it.

It was now moving towards her.

A Detective's Dictionary

Clue /klu/ *n.*
anything that the cops miss.
From *clew*, a ball of thread.
[OE *Cliwen*]

Clue'less *adj*
the cops.

Clue in *v. slang*
to inform the cops of one's
discoveries (not advised).

Chapter Eight
The Lurker in the Dark

Perhaps Bonnie had made a mistake by leaving
Grampa Banks sleeping in the van. Perhaps she had
made a mistake by leaving Warboys in the corridor.
The caretaker might be no good at sneaking, but she
looked like she might be quite handy when it came to
bopping ne'er-do-wells on the head. It was very dark
in the storeroom. How was she supposed to freeze
the intruder to the spot if they could not even see her
expression for freezing people to the spot?

Bonnie had to stay focused. The intruder did not
know she was there, and that gave her an advantage.
As the *scuffle-shuffle* sound grew louder, she

86

crouched down behind an old cleaning trolley. It looked like a small wooden cabinet on wheels, roughly the same size as the detective Montgomery Bonbon. Bonnie's first thought was to squeeze inside, but the cabinet was locked. Thinking fast, she wedged herself ever so neatly between the trolley and a nearby shelf.

Bonnie often found that her small stature was a disadvantage. Grown-ups did not always take small people as seriously as they took tall people. This was a good example of why adults should not be in charge of anything. But right now, Bonnie was glad to be small.

The tread of the intruder grew closer and closer. Not the uneven click-clack of high heels. Not the **clomp-clomp** of coppers' boots. Not the *flip-flop* of flip-flops. Bonnie tried to focus on the sound. What was the *scuffle-shuffle* telling her? A soft sole … like rubber?

As she crouched in the pitch-dark, the intruder's steps had become Bonnie's entire universe. Now they could be no more than three paces away. Two paces. One. Would there be enough light? Was she about to see the shadowy outline of the museum's inside person? She gripped the trolley tightly and tried to squeeze herself even smaller.

"Oi!" came a loud and groggy voice from the alleyway outside. "What the bloomin' heck's going on 'ere?!"

There were many things Bonnie loved about Grampa Banks, and many things that made him an excellent detective's assistant. His talent for blundering in at exactly the wrong moment and shouting loudly was not one of those many things. She heard the intruder skitter and panic, charging away from her now, towards the side door.

"Halt! *Arrêtez!* Stop!" she shouted in Montgomery Bonbon's most irresistibly commanding voice. Somehow her body had converted all the fear she had been bottling up into fury – she could not come so close to catching the crook and then let them get away!

With all her pent-up anger, she shoved the cleaning trolley in what she hoped was the direction of the intruder. It *squeak-squeak-squawked* across the storeroom and bounced off a filing cabinet with a resounding clang.

"Yer! Gerrout of it!" slurred a very sleepy Grampa Banks as the intruder ducked past him and vanished into the Widdlington night. Her grandfather's eyes were still half-closed when Bonnie reached him. A moment later, Warboys was on the scene.

"Did you see them, Banks? Banks, it is most urgent!" demanded Bonnie.

Grampa Banks blinked his drooping eyelids slowly.

"Please to be telling me that you saw the intruder's face!" Bonnie was almost shaking him.

Grampa Banks gave a huge sigh and opened his eyes. Wide. He stared hard at Bonnie, then at Warboys. Bonnie held her breath as Grampa Banks appeared to be about to speak.

"Yes, please..." he muttered, as his eyes rolled around to Warboys's kettle. "Milk and two sugars, if you're making one."

Half an hour later, Inspector Sands was striding up and down the alley next to the museum and poking things with her pen again. She did not look pleased to have been woken up in the middle of the night. Her normally rock-hard bun was loose, and chunks of hair were sticking out at funny angles.

Bonnie might have found it amusing, had she not been so frustrated. She went over what had happened again and again until she felt like twisting her moustache off. There was absolutely no sign of the Widdlington Eagle in the turret room. After examining the place inch by inch, she would have sworn that the eagle really had been stolen.

Except *someone* had just broken in, so *something* important still had to be in the museum. Could they have sneaked the eagle out under Grampa Banks's nose, or was it still hidden inside, somewhere no one had thought to look?

With much cajoling, Montgomery Bonbon had managed to persuade Inspector Sands that a thorough search was (a) necessary; and (b) Inspector Sands's idea.

"Seen this, Bonbon?" she asked. Inspector Sands was squatting near the pile of wet mush on the paving stones that used to be a newspaper.

"Looks like your whatsisname – *intruder* – skidded right through the middle of *The Widdler*."

Inspector Sands was … right. Something about that sentence felt deeply wrong to Bonnie. But it was true: the proof was there in front of her. The intruder's foot had splodged through the middle of the newspaper when they fled.

Bonnie pulled out her magnifying glass, prompting a loud "Oh, here he goes!" from Inspector Sands. Unfortunately the newspaper had been too wet and the intruder moving too fast to leave a clear impression. All Bonnie could make out was *The Widdler*'s headline: *Councillor Suspended Over Sinkhole*. She thought that sounded pretty dangerous, but it did not help with her case.

She was not going to be able to identify the intruder using such a smeared footprint. Still, Bonnie had been so distracted by the chase that she had missed a clue. Worse still, Inspector Sands had noticed it!

Tonight was shaping up to be a disaster.

Bonnie was about to put the magnifying glass away, when something else caught her attention. *The Widdler* often came with flyers promising discounts at local shops, or offering to replace all the windows in your house for no more than the cost of several windows. This edition included a flyer for the annual Widdlington Fayre, smooshed into the floor by the rain. The print was smudged and hard to read, but Bonnie could make out a few words:

> performance by St Hilaria's church choir...
> soloists Oliver Munday and Dana Hornville ...

Oliver Munday and Dana Hornville? There could not be many Hornvilles in a place the size of Widdlington. Could Dana be the spooky girl Bonnie had seen floating around the museum after the murder: Herman Hornville's daughter?

No one Bonnie had spoken to so far had admitted
knowing Oliver outside his job at the museum. If
Dana and Oliver sang in the same choir, perhaps
Dana knew something that was relevant to the case?
Perhaps she had her own reasons for wanting Oliver
Munday out of the way? Could Oliver and Dana have
been rivals?

Bonnie needed to know more.

"Come on, Bonbon. You doing the crossword
down there or what?" grumbled the inspector.

Bonnie straightened up, making the
"Heeeurch!" noise that Grampa Banks
made every time he stood up. Her back
might not have clicked, but something
else did. A wandering loose end. A *clew*.

"The kettle…" she said slowly.

"You what?" asked
Inspector Sands,
but Bonnie was
already padding
away over to
Warboys.

"Your kettle," she began, "please to be reminding me, what is so special about it?"

"I told you already. It went a-wandering." Warboys gestured wildly with the kettle once again, so that Bonnie, Grampa Banks and Inspector Sands could see it. Drawing a very deep breath, the caretaker launched into her story.

"It stopped working a week and a half ago. Faulty appliances are dangerous. Very dangerous. I have a responsibility to the museum. So I took it to my workshop. That's private, my workshop. No one's s'posed to go in there except me. Won't even have one of them horrible stuffed things."

Inspector Sands nodded impatiently.

"That's that, I thought to myself. End of story. Until this afternoon. After all the hoo-ha, I managed to get the lights back on. You lot was all yelling and shouting. And there it sat, plain as day. Somehow this kettle had found its way back into the staffroom!"

Bonnie suspected from the caretaker's expression that this was the most she had ever said in one go.

She looked like she had just wrestled a dolphin. There was a moment of silence while they tried to make sense of the caretaker's strange tale.

"What a load of old horseradish!" scoffed Inspector Sands. "I'm investigating a murder here. I don't have time for Kevin the Travelling Kettle. You're a time-waster." She jabbed a finger towards Warboys, and then rounded on Bonnie and Grampa Banks. "And you're a pair of time-wasters, Bonbon and Mr Thingy. Go home! Leave police work to the professionals."

Sands started to stride back towards the police car parked at the entrance to the alley. She turned around sharply and, walking backwards, added, "That means us!"

Just as she turned back to the police car, Inspector Sands plonked an oversized boot right in the middle of the mushy *Widdler*. Before anyone could react, she skidded towards the parked police car and plunged head first through its open window. The siren came on, blisteringly loud in the night. Curtains started to twitch as sleepy Widdlingtonians tried to work out what the fuss was all about.

"Drive, Simon! Drive!" yelled Sands, wriggling into the passenger seat like an embarrassed stoat, and the police car screeched away.

"She certainly knows how to make an exit," murmured Grampa Banks.

"Most dramatic indeed," agreed Montgomery Bonbon.

Chapter Nine
St Hilaria's Church of the Unfounded Assumption

The people of Widdlington were used to facing two threats: seagulls and olde tea shoppes. You could hardly move around the town centre without tripping over a seagull and landing on an old lady eating an Eccles cake. Worse still, the seagulls and the olde tea shoppes were themselves locked in a timeless struggle for control of Widdlington's scones.

This morning, as the seagulls made off with the latest creation of apprentice baker Alan "Buns" Thompson, the olde tea shoppes were alive with whispers. While iced buns were iced and cream teas were creamed, the people of Widdlington spoke about only one topic: the Blowpipe Killer.

According to the front page of this morning's *Widdler*, Inspector Sands had *almost apprehended the killer during a daring rooftop chase* but interference from a *bungling amateur sleuth, pictured below* had allowed the suspect to escape. Officers were now guarding the Hornville Museum twenty-four hours a day and searching the building for any sign of the missing exhibit.

Bonnie stopped reading and silently crumpled the newspaper into a ball. She had no time to dwell on what had happened at the museum last night. Not when she and Grampa Banks had an investigation to investigate.

The good thing about having an assistant was that you could split up. Detecting sometimes meant doing all kinds of plodding, flat-footed donkey work. Like going door to door, or trawling through the Register of Births, Deaths and Embarrassing Incidents. This did not suit Bonnie. After seven minutes in a reference library, she started to develop a rash.

Fortunately Grampa Banks lived for the dull stuff. Bonnie had asked him to visit the Widdlington Hall of Records to find out everything he could about Oliver Munday. Perhaps the dead man had some dreadful secret in his past, just like the victim in the Great Mannequin Heist. Although, Bonnie had to admit, it did not seem likely. Oliver Munday did not look very much like an arms dealer. Or a legs dealer, for that matter.

Bonnie's sights were set on St Hilaria's choir and Dana Hornville.

Bessie was trundling towards Widdlington Old Town down winding lanes and over humpback bridges. Grampa Banks was driving, dodging seagulls and olde tea shoppes at every turn. Bonnie's mum was in the passenger seat, which meant that Bonnie was stuck in the middle, squeezed between the two of them.

The seating arrangement was not the only thing making Bonnie feel uncomfortable. Her mum had been very excited when Bonnie had started asking questions about St Hilaria's choir at breakfast. And when Liz got excited about something, she *enthused*.

Bonnie had learned long ago that it was better not

to tell lies to her mum. Liz was a very clever person, but she tended to see the world in a way that suited her. If Bonnie told small truths and skipped over big, huge, *massive* Montgomery-Bonbon-shaped truths, her mum tended to fill in the gaps and not ask too many awkward questions. The downside was, every so often Liz tried to get involved.

"I think it's wonderful that you're showing an interest in something that isn't so ... *murdery*," Liz said. "Maybe there'll be other kids your age there. You might make friends. I didn't even know you could sing!"

"I don't know if I can, Mum. I told you, I just want to go along to a rehearsal and have a look."

"I can't believe my daughter is going to be a singer. Such a diva!"

"*Mum!*" yelled Bonnie, but it made no difference. Liz was already belting out "O Holy Night" at maximum volume.

Who knows, maybe her mum was right? This could be the first step on a glittering stairway of musical stardom. She might even make a friend her own age. Both outcomes seemed equally unlikely to Bonnie, but she kept quiet. It was impossible to be anything other than quiet when her mum was singing.

"*Oh, heeeear the angel voooooooices!*"

If Bonnie had been wearing Montgomery Bonbon's moustache, she would have stretched the bristles to try to plug her ears. But she could not turn up at St Hilaria's dressed like the great detective. That would make it obvious she was investigating Oliver Munday's murder, and she wanted to find out about this Dana Hornville without raising any suspicions. Instead she had decided to go undercover as a ten-year-old girl.

Code name: Bonnie Montgomery.

101

Liz was still singing when they dropped Bonnie off outside St Hilaria's Church of the Unfounded Assumption. Grampa Banks gave Bonnie a "please make it stop" look, which made her laugh. Then they trundled away in Bessie, leaving Bonnie alone in the churchyard.

St Hilaria's was one of those crooked old buildings that seemed to have been built by nine people who all hated one another. Cracked red brick mixed with pink and yellow sandstone all the way up to the lopsided

spire. The gravestones were covered with moss and scattered higgledy-piggledy, as if an unusually strong vicar had flung them off the roof. The church organ was warbling into life, rattling the stained-glass windows and making the gargoyles grimace.

Bonnie crossed the uneven flagstones that led up to the entrance. She was definitely in the right place – she could see members of the choir shuffling about inside. Montgomery Bonbon would have marched right in, but Bonnie hesitated.

She was experiencing a sensation known as *not belonging*. The stomach-churning feeling was very familiar to Bonnie from all the after-school activities her mum was always encouraging her to get involved in.

Bonnie took a deep breath. She had a case to solve.

She stepped out of the morning sun and into the church, which seemed to contain Widdlington's entire supply of *cold*. It was dark enough inside that she managed to slip behind a pillar without drawing anyone's attention, then slid quietly into a pew. Bonnie studied the people at the front of the church.

A white-haired woman was pedalling and pummelling the enormous pipe organ, while the choirmaster gathered the young choristers. As they took their positions, they left a sad little gap. That had to be where Oliver usually stood, Bonnie realized. No one laughed or even smiled.

Bonnie scanned their mournful faces and eventually her gaze landed on one she recognized: the girl who had followed Herman Hornville into the museum after the murder. That had to be Dana Hornville. Dressed in a billowy white chorister's tunic, Dana struck Bonnie as even more otherworldly than she had the day before.

The pipe organ burbled into something resembling a tune, and Dana began to sing. Bonnie did not know a lot about music, but she could tell immediately that the young Hornville was talented. Then the rest of the choir joined her. Bonnie could not make out all the lyrics, but it seemed to be a song about someone called Gloria.

Maybe it was the music, or all the dead people six feet beneath her, but Bonnie found herself thinking about her list of suspects: Anton Price, Harriet Spruce, Rashida Zaki … Herman Hornville.

Mr Hornville had seemed so unmoved by news of the crime – could he have recruited a loyal employee like Anton Price to steal the eagle while it was on loan? Or Harriet Spruce? She had been jumpy in the turret room. It seemed like shock at the time, but could it have been guilt for her part in Oliver's murder? Rashida Zaki… Well, apart from seeming vaguely familiar, there was nothing particularly suspicious about the tour guide or her rainbow-coloured waistcoat.

Grampa Banks would probably say Bonnie ought to investigate everyone on her suspect list methodically, one by one. But first she had to find out whether Dana Hornville even belonged on the list. Bonnie kept remembering what Inspector Sands had said back in the turret room: they were looking for someone who could scale a building and still have "enough puff left to use a blowpipe". Having climbed up the museum's fire escape, Bonnie knew she would not have been able to do it. Listening to her solos, Bonnie could tell Dana Hornville had the lungs of a deep-sea diver.

When the rehearsal ended, choristers began to wander off in different directions, like ducks who had finished fighting over a piece of bread. This was Bonnie's moment to strike. She could not simply march up to Dana and start asking questions; she needed to stumble into her *by accident*. It needed to seem natural. It needed to seem casual.

It needed to be cool.

Bonnie had planned to stroll down the aisle looking a little bored, and then act like she had just noticed Dana for the first time. "Oh, are you in the choir?" she would drawl, while inspecting her fingernails. Cool people were always inspecting their fingernails. Bonnie did not know why.

That was her intention, but when she peered back around the pillar, she saw that the choir had all scattered and Dana Hornville was gone. She dashed out from the pew and ran to check the entrance.

There was no sign of Dana in the churchyard.

Bonnie hurried back inside the church and began searching for another exit. St Hilaria's suddenly seemed full of statues, arches and shadowy passageways. She dodged around the stone carvings of church benefactors having a lie down, peered into the dusty alcoves and bent down to look under the pews. With the top of her head scraping the flagstones, she saw … nothing. No sign of Dana Hornville.

Then came a voice.

"Have you lost something?"

Chapter Ten
Dana Hornville

"I said, have you lost something?"

Bonnie could not see who the voice belonged to, but she knew instantly who was behind her. Being caught with her head under a pew was not *exactly* how she had planned to meet Dana Hornville. Gravity and embarrassment worked as a team, and blood rushed to her face. She pulled herself upright too quickly, her head feeling like a gigantic radish. No amount of Bonnie inspecting her fingernails was going to make this seem cool.

Dana Hornville looked at her quizzically.

"I … um…" Bonnie began.

Dana might have been a little older than Bonnie; she was definitely taller. She wore a pair of glasses with tinted lenses. She had removed her tunic and was now wearing her normal clothes, which meant that she was dressed like she was on her way to Queen Victoria's funeral. Her hair looked like someone had been paid to make it look the way it looked.

"I saw you watching us during the rehearsal," said Dana, perching on a marble tomb that looked marginally more comfortable than the pews. "You're a bit weird, aren't you?"

Bonnie was not sure how to react. It was like finding out a vampire thought you were a bit creepy.

"That's OK. I like weird." Dana held out her hand. "Dana Hornville."

Bonnie wiped a clammy palm on her knee before shaking Dana's hand.

"I'm Bonnie. I dropped my..." Bonnie tried to think of something she could have dropped under the pew, but her brilliant detective brain was better at spotting lies than thinking of them. A dog? A basketball? A jam sandwich?

"You can stop shaking my hand now."

"Jam sandwich," agreed Bonnie.

"Are you interested in joining the— Hold on
a minute…" When Dana narrowed her eyes, her
expensive-looking glasses seemed to squint with them.
"Have we met before?"

"No!" said Bonnie, rather too loudly. The word
echoed into the corners of the church and bounced
around the rafters. She waited for the sound to die
away before continuing in a much quieter voice.
"No, I don't think so."

"Which school do you go to?"

"Brushley Park School. Everybody calls it Loo Brush Park."

"Why?" asked Dana.

"It's ... sort of a joke," murmured Bonnie, who was starting to think she was the one being interrogated. She needed to ask Dana a question.

"Where do you go?" she said. "To school, I mean?"

"Saint Heriburga's School for Girls," replied Dana.

Bonnie tried not to say it.

She *really* tried not to say it.

She said it.

"You could call it Saint Hairy Burgers."

Dana blinked at her through tinted glasses. There was a pause that seemed to make the cold church even colder. Dana blinked twice more, then her shoulders started to shake, her lips began to twitch, and she burst out laughing.

"Saint ... Hairy ... BURGERS!" she gasped between peals of laughter.

Bonnie could not help enjoying the effect her little joke had on Dana.

"That is *hilarious*," snorted Dana, taking off her glasses to wipe her eyes. "I'm going to use that."

Dana placed her glasses back on her nose, and suddenly it was as if she had never been laughing. Her serious expression returned, and she fixed Bonnie with a stare, frowning as though she were trying to solve a maths problem in her head.

"I definitely know you from *somewhere*," she said.

"No, I don't think—"

"The museum!" Dana snapped her fingers. "That's it! You were there yesterday when … when it happened."

For a second, Bonnie felt like she was sinking down into the church crypt. She needed to come up with a lie quickly, and she could not afford to *jam sandwich* this situation. She reminded herself that a good lie stays as close to the truth as possible. Hoping her face did not look as panicked as she felt, she answered.

"I was … er… I was there with my grampa," she managed. "Downstairs. I didn't see anything."

"How could you have? The police wouldn't let anyone in the room where it happened. Apart from that detective. What's his name? Mandeville Fudge?"

"Bonbon," said Bonnie as a wave of relief crashed over her. Dana was not quite as observant as she had feared. "I think he's called Montgomery Bonbon."

"Gosh, it's all so horrid, isn't it? And in a way, it was all my fault, you know," said Dana, sliding off the tomb and walking along the central aisle of the church, absent-mindedly pulling Bonnie after her. "You see, I helped dear old Ollie get that job in the first place."

Bonnie knew that Dana's father was rich. And she knew, in theory, that rich people said things like *gosh* and *horrid* and *dear old Ollie*, but actually hearing it was a little bit overwhelming.

Dana must have noticed the look on her face. "Of course, you don't know. Ollie was a member of the choir here at St Hilaria's. I persuaded Father to take him on as a security guard. The Hornville is our museum."

She added this last sentence as an afterthought, as if the museum were a pair of slippers she had forgotten she owned.

"Ollie was saving up to study music at the Sorbet Conservatoire, and I wanted to help. He was ever so talented, you know. I think he even bagged another job on the side while he was working at the museum. Everything seemed to be going well. It's so sad!"

After a shaky start, Bonnie's interrogation was going surprisingly smoothly. Dana seemed to like talking. Bonnie did not want to mess it up by pressing her subject too hard, but she absolutely *had* to know more.

"Do you know anything about what happened to Ollie … ver? Oliver?"

"I wish I did. The first thing I knew about it was Father telephoning the police. Then we dashed over the street to the museum, and I found out that he was … was…" Dana took a shaky breath. "Oh, but I shouldn't be bothering you with all this, should I? Father always says I am far too gloomy. Even … morbid," she added, resting her hand on a carved marble skull. "Kids aren't supposed to take an interest in death and murder and all that rot."

"I'm interested," said Bonnie, "in *all* that rot."

"You are, aren't you?"

Dana thought for a moment, and then produced a small white card, seemingly out of nowhere. She stuck it under Bonnie's nose. It read:

Dana Hornville Esq.
CHORAL SINGER, GRADE 7
PIANIST & COMPETITIVE ARCHER
Flat 3, 142 Museum Street,
Widdlington Old Town

"Do you want to be friends?"

"What?" asked Bonnie, hypnotized by the dazzlingly crisp letters on the card.

"It's OK; you don't have to decide now." Dana pressed the card into Bonnie's hand. "Just drop by if you feel like it. Find out more about the choir or whatever."

Dana squinted her glasses again. "Oh, and, Bonnie?"

"Yes?"

"You're still shaking my hand."

IMPORTANT
When being COOL remember:
close eyelids 20%
dry sweaty palms
Inspect finger nails
LEAN...
on something without wheels
or this happens...

Chapter Eleven
A Grave Encounter

St Hilaria's Church was empty now, apart from
Bonnie Montgomery and several statues that were too
embarrassed to look her in the eye. After the conversation
with Dana, her thoughts were like wind-up toys, whizzing
around crazily and banging into the walls of her skull.

Did I say something stupid? I think I said
something stupid. What kind of kid has a business
card? Should I have a business card? What was Ollie's
side job? I mean, what was *Oliver's* side job?

Bonnie closed her eyes and took a deep breath, her
cheeks still flushed and sizzling. She could not be sure
whether she had interviewed Dana or whether Dana

had interviewed her. However, she had learned a few things about the murder victim, and at least she had spoken to a potential suspect face to face. Even if her own face had been so hot you could have toasted marshmallows on it.

She found it hard to imagine a kid being responsible for such a cold-blooded murder, but Bonnie knew better than anyone that it was a mistake to underestimate children. Her instincts told her that, like a fingerprint on a door handle or a spot of blood on a carpet, the youngest Hornville was not to be ignored.

She stepped outside. The Widdlington sky had filled with hazy white cloud during choir practice, and the sun made the churchyard bright and shadowless. She knew places like this were supposed to be eerie. Graveyards were the kind of places other children ran past screaming. But Bonnie had always felt strangely at home among the graves. She listened to the rustling of the trees and the bumbling buzz of fat bumblebees and began to relax. For Bonnie, the headstones around her represented row

after row of closed cases.

She noticed a giant grey ice-cream cone poking out from behind a ragged privet hedge. That meant Bessie was parked near by, and her mum and grampa were waiting for her. She was going to have to come up with an excuse her mum would believe for not going back to choir practice. Bad vibes? Natural disaster? Was there such a thing as athlete's *throat*?

Bonnie's train of thought derailed and plunged into a ravine when a flash of colour caught her eye. When Montgomery Bonbon had first seen Rashida Zaki, the museum guide had been wearing a rainbow-coloured waistcoat. Now Bonnie found herself staring at a rainbow blazer so colourful it looked like one of the stained-glass windows had broken loose. It was Rashida Zaki all right, appearing and disappearing between mossy headstones. She seemed to be talking to someone on her mobile.

Bonnie was very experienced at judging whether things were suspicious or not. She consulted her internal fishy-ometer, which ran all the way from *Hardly Suspicious* to *Definitely a Murderer*, and concluded that making a phone call in a graveyard ranked as *Pretty Suspicious* (just above owning a walking stick that turns into a sword and just below having a twin whom no one ever mentions). Nothing about Rashida had struck Bonnie as particularly suspicious. Yet here she was, making a phone call in a graveyard.

S. Cullen
Crossbone
Rests Here

BLANCH BONE

DEDUN BERRTED

YORICK SCULLY
RIP

Bonnie knew what she *ought* to do: go and tell Grampa Banks everything about Dana Hornville. Then they could interview the remaining suspects one by one – if they didn't both die of boredom first. But what kind of detective could pass up a chance to listen in on a private phone call in such a creepy and mysterious location?

Bonnie knew it was wrong to eavesdrop. She had been told off many times for being nosy and listening in on people's conversations. But when an unsuspicious person acts suspiciously, it is always worth investigating. She made a decision. Her mum and Grampa Banks could wait in Bessie for a little bit longer, while she followed Rashida. But she would have to be very careful. Montgomery Bonbon's outfit was still at home. Bonnie Montgomery was not supposed to be on this particular case.

The long grass whispered as Bonnie darted from headstone to headstone towards Rashida. She ducked behind granite slabs and crumbling obelisks. She crabbed sideways along a bench. She followed the rainbow blazer all the way from *Darling Judith* past *In*

Memory of Dudley Croup and finally *to Beloved Charles Norgood, who went to sleep on the 16th August 1891.*

Bonnie thought that burying someone who had fallen asleep sounded a tiny bit hasty, but she did not have time to worry about it, because just then she heard something that made her freeze.

"…never know exactly what happened," Rashida was saying in her tantalizingly familiar drawl. "But there is no doubt in my mind that Hornville stole the eagle."

Bonnie was too professional to gasp out loud, but she couldn't stop her jaw from dropping. Was Rashida actually investigating the case? Bonnie could not help feeling personally insulted. Did the museum guide not have faith in the deductive powers of the great Montgomery Bonbon? Was she working for Inspector Sands? Was she talking to Inspector Sands right now? Most importantly…

HOW HAD SHE WORKED IT OUT BEFORE BONNIE?

She peered over the carved buttocks of a marble cherub, and listened very, very carefully.

"My research proves that Eudora Potts was the

one who discovered the Widdlington Eagle, *not* Hornville. Hornville took all the credit for the discovery, and sold the eagle to make his fortune."

Bonnie felt like someone had poked a feather in her ear and started tickling her brain. It did not sound like Rashida was talking about Herman Hornville. She had to be talking about *Abelard* Hornville, Herman's incredibly wealthy grandfather.

"I'm now standing in front of a small grave in a forgotten corner of an untended churchyard," continued Rashida. "The name carved in the stone is Eudora Potts. There is no one around. It's easy to imagine that I am the first person in decades to visit Eudora's resting place."

There was something strange about the way she was talking. It did not sound very much like someone making a phone call. When Bonnie's mum made calls, she always said things like, "No way!" and, "He never did!" and, "He's not good for you, Jackie, trust me." Rashida had not said any of those things.

"I hope Eudora would be pleased that, all these years later, someone finally knows the truth. Maybe it's time we forgot about the Abelard Hornvilles of this world and remembered women like Eudora Potts."

Rashida paused for a moment, then added, "That might be a good ending, actually. Maybe go straight from that into: 'This is Madison Garden for *History's Mysterious Mysteries*. Case closed.'"

Realization hit Bonnie like a wet flannel. Rashida was not making a phone call. She was recording a podcast. And that was why Bonnie recognized her voice.

Rashida Zaki was recording Bonnie's *favourite* podcast.

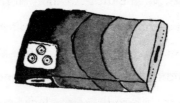

Chapter Twelve
History's Mysterious Mysteries

Bonnie had listened to every single episode of *History's Mysterious Mysteries*. Most of them twice. Some of them thrice. And now she was standing paces away from the woman behind the show.

Stay calm, Bonnie told herself. Play it cool. But it was too late; she was already vaulting over the cherub's marble buttocks in the direction of Rashida Zaki.

"I'M SUCH A HUGE FAN!" she cried in a voice so loud it nearly woke up Beloved Charles Norgood.

Rashida gave a yelp of surprise. She swung round and her expensive-looking phone went flying.

"Gee, kid! Where the heck did you spring from?"
She goggled at Bonnie as if the girl had just leaped up
out of a grave.

"I was hiding behind that statue," confessed
Bonnie, too excited to lie. It was lucky that she was
not dressed as Montgomery Bonbon, otherwise she
might well have blown her cover.

"O-K…"

"I really love *History's Mysterious Mysteries*. It's my favourite podcast. That's why I recognized your voice!" gabbled Bonnie a little too energetically.

"That's … neat." But Rashida's expression said that it was not, in fact, neat. "Hey, were you following me just now?"

"No!" said Bonnie, slamming the brakes on the truth and coming to a screeching halt. "No, never, no. I just came to the churchyard to visit my" – she looked around for support and spotted a nearby grave – "pet hamster." She patted the headstone and tried to look honest.

Rashida frowned at its crumbling lettering. "You had a hamster called Neil Anderson?"

"Yep," said Bonnie.

"The Right Honourable Neil Anderson MP?"

"Y-yes."

"Who died aged … seventy-six?" asked Rashida.

"Mmm-hmm. Fell off his wheel."

They stared at each other in silence for a long moment. Bonnie was a good judge of character, but she could not tell if Rashida was buying it.

Eventually Rashida said, "You're weird, kid."

Why did people keep saying that?

"Listen," the woman continued, "I gotta be somewhere, so…"

Bonnie could tell Rashida was trying to back out of the conversation and she needed to stop her. Bossing suspects around was so much easier when you could just wiggle your moustache.

"Wait, wait!" said Bonnie. "Could I … listen to it? The episode about the Widdlington Eagle?"

"No, I don't think so. It's not finished yet. I'm kind of waiting until the cops figure out who stole the eagle. I guess you heard about that? Apparently they're real close to catching the guy, but some amateur private eye keeps messing things up."

Bonnie felt the enthusiasm draining from her as Rashida continued.

"That bossy guy with the soup-strainer moustache. Is he, like, a local celebrity or something?"

"He's the world's finest detective," Bonnie said stiffly.

"OK, sure, whatever. Hey, did you see what happened to my phone?"

Bonnie *had* seen what happened. The rainbow-coloured device was peeking out from behind Eudora Potts's headstone, next to a wilted bunch of petrol station flowers.

"I think it landed … over there, in the long grass." Bonnie pointed somewhere else entirely. She was lying, a little more convincingly now, because she wanted time to ask a few more questions.

"So … did you take the job at the Hornville because you wanted to investigate the history of the eagle undercover?" Bonnie asked casually, rooting around in the long grass and old leaves.

"Actually, I've worked there for a few months. I only heard about the eagle when it came over from the States. Then I started interviewing a whole bunch of people: my boss, Harriet Spruce, Eudora's last living relative, Anton Price, the museum docent at the NJMFNOS."

"The … nuhjumpfnoz?"

"Yeah, the NJMFNOS. The New Jersey Museum for Neat Old Stuff. They bought the eagle from Abelard Hornville for a *ton* of money back in 1931.

That's what's so nuts about the whole thing. If Eudora hadn't been working for him, Hornville might've spent the rest of his life knee-deep in mud, digging up clay pipes. Without Eudora Potts, it wouldn't even be called the Hornville Mus— Hey, wait a sec..." Rashida stopped searching for her phone and turned to face Bonnie. "How did you know I worked at the museum?"

"I must have ... erm ... seen you while visiting," fumbled Bonnie.

"I *knew* you were following me!"

"No, I— Oh look, it's your phone!" said Bonnie, pointing towards the rainbow-coloured case.

"Who do you work for?" demanded Rashida, snatching up the phone. She stalked towards Bonnie. For someone wearing a rainbow blazer, she certainly looked fierce. "*Mysterio Cast? Curiouser and Curiousest?* Which podcast wants to steal my story?"

"I promise, I – I..." Bonnie stammered, backing away from Rashida. She expected to bump into cold stone. Instead she collided with something soft and familiar.

"Is this one bothering you?" asked Liz Montgomery cheerfully, plonking her hands heavily on Bonnie's shoulders. "I'm sorry; she does tend to be a bit nosy." Liz wiggled the tip of Bonnie's nose.

"Muuuuum!"

Bonnie felt strongly that the world's finest detective ought to be able to investigate a murder without having their nose wiggled against their will.

"I'm always having to remind her that it's rude to listen in on other people's conversations."

"It's OK," said Rashida, still looking a bit upset. "I'd just like a little privacy, that's all."

"Come on then, young lady!" ordered Bonnie's mum, taking her daughter by the arm and marching her briskly towards Bessie. "Your grampa is driving me to an appointment with Guru Jonathan Jonathan."

Bonnie had to skip to keep up. "Wait!" Skip. "Mum!" Skip. "Just!" Skip. "One!" Skip. "More!" Skip. "Question!"

But it was too late. Rashida Zaki, aka Madison Garden, was soon just a grumpy-looking rainbow smudge in the distance. And, in no time at all, Bonnie was squeezed into Bessie's middle seat, turning everything she had just heard over and over in her mind.

Eudora Potts … Abelard Hornville…

She found it hard to imagine that Oliver Munday's murder could be connected with something from nearly a hundred years ago. On the other hand, keeping the past alive was exactly what museums were for.

And there was another thing. Bonnie had noticed something that Rashida had not: the withered bundle of petrol station flowers lying behind Eudora Potts's headstone.

Could that mean *someone else* had visited Eudora's grave recently?

"Case closed." That was what Rashida had said. But Bonnie's intuition told her that the case of the Widdlington Eagle was far from closed. Like Grampa Banks's suitcase when they went to Rittlin's Holiday Camp, it had burst wide open, spilling secrets and underpants everywhere.

As Bessie pulled away from St Hilaria's, the church clock struck.

GlorrOrrorrong!

It was one in the afternoon. Squidged in between her mother and grampa, Bonnie realized that this meant a window was opening at Widdlington Police Station. (Not an actual window: a window of *opportunity*. The actual windows had all been sealed shut by the council to muffle the sound of Inspector Sands.)

By now, Widdlington Constabulary should have received a crime lab report about the type of poison used to kill Oliver Munday. And, since Montgomery Bonbon had been caught trying to bribe his way into the lab last Michaelmas, there was only one way Bonnie was going to get that information.

A Crisp Run.

"Grampa Banks?" began Bonnie tentatively. "Once we've dropped Mum off, can we go on a Crisp Run?"

"A crisp run?" said Bonnie's mum with a note of excitement. "You know you can always join me on my six o'clock morning jog!"

Bonnie loved her mum, but she made detecting difficult sometimes.

"No, no! I don't want to jog – bleurgh!" she said, before Liz had a chance to start enthusing. "I mean a *Crisp Run*. Crisps, like snacks." Bonnie wiggled her eyebrows meaningfully.

"If you're peckish, there might be an old lemon sherbet in the glove compartment," said Grampa Banks. He was concentrating on the road and could not see Bonnie's eyebrows.

"No," said Bonnie firmly. "I fancy crisps. A *Crisp Run*."

Bonnie wiggled her eyebrows so hard she thought they were going to come loose and drop into the footwell.

Grampa Banks must have heard the wiggling this time. "Ooooh," he said, very slowly. "A CRISP Run. Good idea."

"So it's settled, then? A Crisp Run?" asked Bonnie.

"A Crisp Run," agreed Grampa Banks.

"You two spend too much time together," muttered Bonnie's mum.

Chapter Thirteen

The Crisp Run

Widdlington Police Station was a drab, grey-brown building with a flat roof. The windows were tiny squares, spaced out so that passers-by could see very little of the inside. Bonnie always got the impression that the architect had started out designing a prison and changed their mind at the last minute.

Montgomery Bonbon and his assistant were lurking around the back entrance to the station; Bonnie's mum had been safely dropped off at Guru Jonathan Jonathan's sanctuary. She was having her chakras opened. Or closed. Bonnie could never remember which.

Grampa Banks had returned from the Widdlington Hall of Records with a little notebook full of facts about Oliver Munday, and this was their first chance to discuss his findings in private.

"As far as I can tell, our Oliver was raised by his aunt. She passed away a couple of years ago."

"Hmm." Bonnie twirled her moustache thoughtfully. "Did he have any convictions?"

"I'm afraid not. Clean as a whistle," replied Grampa Banks.

"What about the aunt?" she asked hopefully.

He flipped back a few pages and checked his notes. "Clean as a whistle."

"Shame."

Grampa Banks flipped onwards. "Oh, and he went to Brushley Park, just like you."

Bonnie stuck her tongue out at the mention of her school. "Any … detentions?"

Flip-flip-flip.

"Clean as a whistle."

Bonnie frowned. Every avenue Grampa Banks had investigated ended up hitting the same roadblock: "Clean as a whistle." It did not seem right to Bonnie to sum up a young man's whole life with a list of facts. It seemed so … boring.

Perhaps Oliver Munday had dreamed of travelling to Paris to study music! He might have married a Parisian waiter and gone hot-air ballooning over the Alps. He might have discovered a new kind of yodelling, ended all wars and stopped them from serving rice pudding at Loo Brush Park.

Well, maybe not that exactly. But the point was, Oliver Munday once had had the potential to do anything he wanted. And someone had taken that away from him. Montgomery Bonbon was going to catch the person responsible. And to do that, Bonnie needed to know exactly what killed him.

That was where the Crisp Run came in.

A successful detective needs to keep the local police onside. Sometimes they need to share information or deal with the fiddly business of arresting a murderer. This was tricky for Bonnie, because Inspector Sands had banned Montgomery Bonbon from setting foot inside Widdlington Police Station. On pain of catapult.

Bonnie did not believe Widdlington Constabulary actually owned their own catapult, never mind one that was large enough to twang a ten-year-old dressed as a middle-aged private investigator. But Grampa Banks had expressly forbidden her from testing that hypothesis. Since the inspector would not freely share information about the case, Bonnie and Grampa Banks had no choice but to employ a manoeuvre. This was why Montgomery Bonbon and his assistant were loitering outside the station.

The Crisp Run was about to begin.

"Two prawn cocktail, three sizzly bacon, one cheesy pickle, one bag of salty nuts."

Bonnie and Grampa Banks watched as Constable Simon emerged from the back door.

140

His eyes were half-closed as he recited the other officers' crisp orders to himself.

"Two prawn cocktail, three sizzly bacon, one cheesy pickle, one bag of salty nuts."

The police station's tiny sealed windows were doing their job – Bonnie could see but not hear Inspector Sands. The inspector appeared to be *clomp, clomp, clomping* from desk to desk, looking for people to yell at. Her hair was even more frazzled than the night before. She did not seem like someone who would take kindly to being brought the wrong flavour of crisp.

"Two prawn cocktail – oh, bother!"

Constable Simon had spotted Bonnie and Grampa Banks. They fell into step with him, one on either side of the young officer. He was speed-walking, on autopilot, towards Cheapies, the corner shop with the largest selection of crisps on the east coast.

"Good afternoon, Constable," said Montgomery Bonbon in an excessively polite voice.

"Afternoon, lad," added Grampa Banks.

"TWO PRAWN COCKTAIL –

good afternoon – THREE SIZZLY BACON –
gentlemen – ONE CHEESY PICKLE – how can I –
ONE BAG OF SALTY NUTS – be of service?" said
Constable Simon, sweating with concentration.

"We were wondering how the investigation, it is
proceeding?" began Bonnie.

"Sorry – PRAWN COCKTAIL – I can't –
SIZZLY BACON – tell you anything – CHEESY
PICKLE – Inspector's orders – SALTY NUTS."

The constable's eyes were completely closed now.

"*Mein ami*, naturally you could not be *expickled* to disobey orders."

"Perish the thought, old prawn," chipped in Grampa Banks.

"But perhaps you could *cocktail* us one thing?"

"No – PICKLY BACON – can't – CHEESY PRAWN – salty nut's orders."

Bonnie was glad to be back in Montgomery Bonbon's raincoat. Everything went much more smoothly when Bonbon was on the case; he never got tongue-tied or made a fool of himself. She had Simon completely discombobulated. It was time to strike.

"You have been sworn to the secrecy about the poison used by the killer, *ja*?"

"That's right – VERY RARE – not a word – EXOTIC PLANT – my lips – FROM SOUTH AMERICA – are sealed – SALTY NUTS."

"Then we bid you *au revoir*," said Bonnie.

Bonnie and Grampa Banks stopped dead, and Constable Simon raced away in the direction of Cheapies.

"Mind how you go," called Grampa Banks cheerily.

"One bag of salty poison," muttered Constable Simon as he disappeared around the corner.

"A very rare and exotic plant from South America," repeated Grampa Banks. "Does that mean anything to you, old man?"

"A clue is being a clue, *mein ami*," said Bonnie wisely. It sounded better than saying, "*Non*."

Grampa Banks gave a long whistle. "Peppermint tea, love?"

"Yes please!"

There had been a murder in the olde tea shoppe. A custard cream biscuit lay on a lace tablecloth – dead. Three teaspoons jingled over from the other side of the table, where they discovered that the sugar cube the victim had been guarding was gone. Moments later, a piece of millionaire's shortbread arrived on the scene, accompanied by his daughter, a small jug of cream.

Bonnie let out a long sigh, and then ate the sugar cube that represented the Widdlington Eagle. Grampa Banks coughed a cough of disapproval from behind today's edition of *The Widdler*.

"So," she began, for the umpteenth time, "we've got three people who all say they were somewhere else when the murder happened. And we now know one of them has a secret identity. That's Pretty Suspicious, isn't it?"

Grampa Banks looked at Bonnie over *The Widdler*, raising a quizzical eyebrow. "Is it, old bean?"

Grampa Banks's eyebrow was right. Having a secret identity did not make Rashida Zaki a murderer. Perhaps she had to use a different name in her podcast to prevent super-fans from jumping out at her in graveyards. People love true crime stories, thought

Bonnie. Could Rashida have staged the theft to make the Eudora Potts mystery more exciting?

Bonnie wiggled spoons and slid teacups around on the table as she tried to make sense of everything.

Rashida had reminded her that the eagle was being loaned to the Hornville Museum from the NJMFNOS for the first time. That gave the millionaire's shortbread a good motive – sorry – gave *Herman Hornville* a good motive. Maybe he resented the fact that his grandfather had sold the eagle and decided he wanted it for himself? Could he have asked his daughter to climb up to the roof that day? Could she have lost a hairpin in the process? It was possible, yet no matter how many times Bonnie tried to picture Dana wearing a flowery hairpin, she failed.

But *someone* had lost a hairpin on the fire escape. Bonnie had seen Rashida climb down it, but Rashida's hair was short and spiky. And Anton barely had enough hair to pin. Perhaps Warboys had been right when she said it belonged to Harriet. Had Ms Spruce been out there on the roof in secret? Would she be able to make sense of that code Bonnie had found?

61 and *1E*. There was something about those numbers that just did not seem right.

Bonnie sighed again.

Grampa Banks gave her a sympathetic smile and folded over *The Widdler* to show her an artist's impression of the Blowpipe Killer. Bonnie was pretty certain she knew who the artist was, because the suspect had been given evil glowing eyes. And horns. And stink lines.

Thanks to Constable Simon, Bonnie knew the poison that killed Oliver came from a rare South American plant. Bonnie was surprised Inspector Sands had not drawn the Blowpipe Killer with a poncho and llama. But it did not help Bonnie make sense of the murder or the intruder at the museum last night. She looked down at the table. It perfectly resembled the inside of her brain right now.

It was a total mess.

Bonnie sighed. She was about to sneak another sugar cube, when Grampa Banks plonked the newspaper down on top of everything and gave a triumphant "Aha!"

Bonnie recognized that sound. It was the sound of inspiration striking. But the inspiration seemed to have missed her and struck Grampa Banks. That was not supposed to happen. Perhaps they were sitting in the wrong seats.

"What is it?" she asked eagerly, but Grampa Banks just grinned and tapped the newspaper with a gnarly old finger. Bonnie leaned over the cheap grey paper, with its fuzzy, smelly ink, and read:

M. BONBON, Please visit 11B SLENDER LANE at your earliest convenience. I rather think you might learn something that will be to your benefit.

Bonnie and Grampa Banks looked at each other. There was something about the old-fashioned way the personal ad was written that made Bonnie think she knew exactly who had placed it. And it was clear this person had more to tell them about what had happened in the turret room.

"Shall I start Bessie?" asked Grampa Banks.

Bonnie crammed the dearly departed custard cream in her mouth and – spraying crumbs across the tablecloth – said, "*Toot sweet!*"

Chapter Fourteen
Slender Lane

The town of Widdlington should never be confused with its bitter rival, Widdling-on-Sea. People from Widdlington read *The Widdler*, whereas people over in Widdling-on-Sea read the *Widdling-on-Sea Bugle*. According to Grampa Banks, a proud

Widdlington man, the *Widdling-on-Sea Bugle* was a cheap and nasty imitation of *The Widdler*. The residents of Widdlington would rather fight a seagull than be

caught reading the *Bugle*. Similarly, the denizens of Widdling-on-Sea would rather fight a seagull than read *The Widdler*, because they love fighting.

Grampa Banks was not best pleased to discover that Slender Lane was in Widdling-on-Sea, but they crossed the River Widdle anyway. Bonnie immediately saw that Slender Lane lived up to its name. It was a narrow passage, paved with smooth old flagstones that never saw the sun. The pebble-dashed walls of the buildings on either side looked like lumpy porridge. A few doors and windows opened onto the shady alleyway.

Grampa Banks shook his head and tutted. "I don't like it, old man. It could be a trap."

"*Pardonnez-me, mein ami*," said Bonnie, hamming up Montgomery Bonbon's voice, "but you were being the one who suggested coming here."

"Exactly! I'm always falling for traps. Remember the Case of the Lost Lobster Pot?"

Bonnie scowled. "I thought we were never going to get you out of that pot." She cleared her throat. "But you are suspicious simply because we are being in Widdling-on-Sea, *non*?"

"*Non*, I mean…" Grampa Banks lowered his voice in case any of the locals heard him. "Yes!"

"Well, if it is being a trap, Montgomery Bonbon, he will discover who is setting the trap, *ja*?"

Grampa Banks sighed and reluctantly said, "*Ja*."

With a grin, Bonnie took off into the narrow street. In the old tea shoppe the case had seemed impossibly muddled. Now she was back on the trail, everything seemed clearer. If Slender Lane held any clues, Montgomery Bonbon would find them.

Her eyes were on the doors as she hurried down the lane. Number 8, number 9, number 10, number 11A, number 12, number … hold on…

Bonnie doubled back and checked again: 8, 9, 10, 11A, 12. Slowly and carefully she checked the wall behind her, but there was no door to be found. There seemed to be no such place as 11B Slender Lane. Grampa Banks caught up with her, looking equally perplexed. He was holding his old camera close to his chest, as if afraid that a Widdling-on-Sea hoodlum might run up and take a photo of him with it.

"Tread carefully, old man. They're always up to

funny stuff around here," he whispered.

Bonnie studied the bumpy whitewashed wall between number 11A and number 12. And there it was, mounted all alone on the wall: a doorbell labelled 11B. A doorbell with no door.

"*Regardez*: 11B."

Click, FLASH, grrr…

"How odd." Grampa Banks frowned. "Shall I press it?"

"Go on, then," replied Bonnie. Grown-ups had to be allowed *some* fun.

Grampa Banks buzzed the buzzer, and Bonnie heard a sound like an electric woodpecker coming from inside. Then silence. Followed by more silence. And then a third silence that lasted just a little too long, before being broken by the *ponk-ponk-ponk* of someone tapping on glass.

The sash window in front of Bonnie slid open with a screech. She was not surprised to see Anton Price standing inside. Who else would

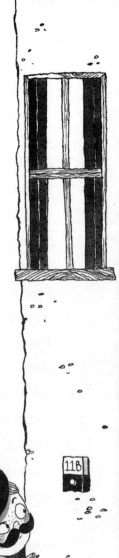

153

place a personal ad in a newspaper but the Hornville Museum's restorer – the man who looked like a rare old museum piece himself? Anton produced a crooked wooden stool and painstakingly manoeuvred it out of the window and onto the flagstones beneath.

"I'm ever so glad you saw my note," he said. "Come in! Come in! Please do."

It seemed a little strange, but Montgomery Bonbon was a man of the world, and was not going to be scared off by a wobbly stool. Not after he had braved the Hornville's fire escape. Bonnie and Grampa Banks climbed awkwardly through the window into Anton Price's cramped hallway. The ceiling was so low that Anton had to hunch over, and Grampa Banks ended up wearing a lampshade like a hat.

"Number 11 used to be one property, you see," explained Anton Price, "but the landlord divided it into two and next door got the … um … well … they got the door. This is called a maisonette. Very reasonably priced, though!" he added brightly, wedging the front window closed.

"Most interesting," said Bonnie, trying to give the

impression of admiring Anton's home. Her own house was hardly big, but this place was *tiny*. Bonnie's mum often said that there was not enough room to swing a cat in 321 Dead End. Bonnie had never understood why anyone would want to swing a cat in their house in the first place. It seemed terribly unfair on the cat. Whatever Liz meant, there certainly was not enough room to swing a cat in 11B Slender Lane. Unless you wanted a lot of broken ornaments and a very angry cat.

"Please, do come upstairs and join me in the sitting room."

The landlord's new wall seemed to run right up the middle of Anton's staircase, so Bonnie and Grampa Banks had to turn sideways to climb it. Sidling up, one by one, they got a close-up view of Anton's old photographs: tea-coloured pictures of the Hornville Museum and ghostly images of people wearing flat caps, victory rolls and serious expressions.

The sitting room was another narrow room, only a little wider than Bonnie's arm span. Anton swept aside a pile of old *Widdlers* and ushered his guests onto one half of a leather sofa. He did not sit on the

other half of the sofa, because there was no other half.

Bonnie could see Grampa Banks's trigger finger resting on the shutter of his camera. She knew he had to be dying to take some snaps of Anton Price's weird little house, but she hoped he would do it surreptitiously. She did not want to upset their host. At least, not until she had found out why Montgomery Bonbon had been invited in the first place.

"Tea?" asked Anton. Without waiting for an answer, he picked up a fine china teapot and poured out three dainty little cups. He then took a seat in an armchair by the open window at the opposite end of the room. By some optical illusion, the unusual shape of their host's home made it seem like he was sitting very, very far away from them. He smiled a thin but welcoming smile, and it struck Bonnie that he seemed to suit his tiny little world. He sipped his tea, and a gentle sea breeze wafted the curtains around him. The scene was a quiet and placid one.

Even a mind as brilliant as Montgomery Bonbon's could not have guessed that the Blowpipe Killer was, at that moment, preparing to strike.

Chapter Fifteen

The Blowpipe Killer

"You have a very beautiful home," said Grampa Banks politely, almost sliding off Anton's half a sofa. Grampa Banks was very good at knowing what to say to people, even when it was obviously not true.

"Oh, thank you, Mr...?"

"Banks," he answered, shifting his bottom slightly and knocking over a lamp.

"Thank you, Mr Banks. You're most kind. It's ... it's not large, but..."

Anton trailed off again, with a flutter of his bony fingers. It occurred to Bonnie that Anton was a little like Barry Houdini, a local crook who had escaped from jail thirty-seven times – he was better at starting sentences than finishing them.

The teacup Anton was holding had a small chip in the base. Bonnie would not have noticed it, but Anton kept absent-mindedly scratching at it with one of his long, clean fingernails. The restorer was still smiling, but behind the smile he seemed nervous. On edge. This is a person, thought Bonnie, who is holding on to a secret.

Anton seemed to be waiting for Montgomery Bonbon to speak, so Bonnie tried to get things moving.

"So…" she began.

"So," agreed Anton.

"We were reading your notice in the newspaper…"

"Mmm!" He nodded.

Silence settled on them again.

Anton folded and unfolded his arms. He crossed and uncrossed his legs. He opened his mouth as if to speak … and then wordlessly took another sip of tea. Bonnie gazed around for anything that might spark a conversation and spotted what looked like a retirement card on Anton's coffee table.

"Ah, you are retiring, Monsieur?"

"Mmm? Oh, yes. Yes, of course. Today should have been my last day."

Bonnie was not a fan of greetings cards in general. Cards for girls tended to have princesses on them, which she hated. Cards for boys tended to have footballs on them, which she also hated. Her mum usually got cards that announced it was wine o'clock, which Bonnie hated because wine o'clock was not a real time. Grampa Banks usually got cards that said things like *You are EXTREMELY old, you old DINGBAT*, which Bonnie thought was pretty funny, actually.

Anton's retirement card simply said: *On your retirement. Thank you for everything* and appeared to be signed by everyone at the museum.

"With all the unpleasantness, I almost forgot about it," continued Anton. "Oliver was such a nice young man. He picked out the card, you know."

Bonnie waited for him to continue, but another awkward pause yawned between them, as vast as the sinkhole that had swallowed the Widdling-on-Sea lighthouse. Was Anton testing her? He was certainly testing her patience.

The silence stretched on. Anton quietly *shlooped* his tea and shuffled in his chair, and Bonnie's mind began to wander. Perhaps Grampa Banks was right about this being a trap. Perhaps Anton was working with the Blowpipe Killer, who could be sidling up the stairs behind them at this very moment. Perhaps a cage was about to drop, leaving her and Grampa Banks at the mercy of a murderer.

She risked a quick glance up at the ceiling. No cage, she noted, just flaky paint. She watched a small flake peel off, spiral down in front of her and plop into her cup of tea. Her host saw it too, but he only winced and remained silent.

Anton Price had something to say, but clearly he was not yet ready to explain the reason for his puzzling message in the newspaper. She had to try a different approach.

Wait a minute, she thought. *The Widdler...*

"Tell me, Monsieur Price, have you always been living here in the Widdling-on-Sea?"

"Oh, yes. Yonks. Absolutely yonks…"

"Yonks, you say," said Bonnie, with a meaningful glance at Grampa Banks. "That is the news most interesting." She gestured with her teacup towards Anton's issues of *The Widdler.* "I ask this to you because you appear not to read the *Widdling-on-Sea Bugle,* the newspaper so popular on this side of the Widdle. I think perhaps you are from Widdlington, originally? Like my assistant, Monsieur Banks."

"You know, that's very perceptive!" said Anton, beaming. "You're quite right, Detective. I've lived here for a long time, but in fact, I was born in Widdlington."

It was only a small deduction, but Bonnie could feel her moustache quivering triumphantly. Grampa Banks gave her a congratulatory wink, and nearly slipped off the side of the half a sofa.

There was something else.

Anton was serving tea using a fine china tea set that looked ancient enough to be an antique. It was old, even by comparison with Anton himself, and chipped. It did not look like something Anton, with

163

his modest style of dress, would buy himself. And why had he, a museum restorer, not repaired the chip? Could the fancy china be a treasured memento of a loved one?

It was a gamble but, encouraged by her success, Bonnie decided to take it.

"And the teapot, she belonged to … your mother, *nes pah*?"

Anton's mouth hung open, just for a second.

"No."

Bonnie felt her moustache drooping.

"But it's funny you should say that. It happens to have been my grandmother's, you see. I moved over here after she passed away," Anton told them. "I fell in love with the view."

With another bony flourish, he gestured towards the open window beside him. All Bonnie could see were more windows on the opposite side of Slender Lane. She was a little cross that her deduction had been off, but Anton still seemed impressed.

"You know, you are quite a bit sharper than they said you were in the newspaper," Anton continued.

"I knew I did the right thing by contacting you. You see, I know something … or rather, I think I might… That is to say…"

Anton shuffled about on his chair, the leather making little squeaks and parps. Bonnie tried to think of a polite way of yelling, "GET ON WITH IT!"

"Perhaps a little more tea?" Anton quavered, standing up to pour himself another cup from the teapot on the table in front of him.

Bonnie was ready to scream. But, to her great surprise, Anton did it for her.

"AAAH!"

His shriek was so piercing that Bonnie and Grampa Banks both jumped in fright. Bonnie heard the **Click, FLASH, grrr** of Grampa Banks's camera as Anton's fine china teapot shattered into countless pieces on the rug.

Through a haze of steam, they saw their host shrinking away from some unseen terror: eyes wide, mouth gaping, trousers moist. (With spilled tea, Bonnie hoped.) She was on her feet in an instant, turning her perceptive abilities towards the cowering man, the open window, the tea-stained rug.

"What? Who?" gibbered Anton, stretching a long grey finger towards his armchair.

Bonnie followed his gaze. And there it was. Sticking into the arm of Anton's chair. Precisely where the museum restorer had been sitting a moment earlier.

A still-quivering, red-feathered *dart*.

The Blowpipe Killer had struck again!

Chapter Sixteen
An Impossible Picture

Bonnie came to her senses and dropped to her hands and knees. She swiftly deduced that the blow dart must have been fired through the window beside Anton, zipping through the air with deadly speed and narrowly missing its target. If Anton had stood up even a second later…

The window was still open wide, curtains billowing. A second dart could be on its way at any moment.

"An attempt has been made on the witness's life! It is most important that we—" began Bonnie, before Grampa Banks realized what had just happened, and exploded.

"Stay low! KEEP CAAAAALM!" he yelled.

Bonnie thought she heard at least four extra As in *calm*. Her trusty assistant was clearly not taking his own advice. He barrelled over the half a sofa and charged towards the narrow staircase. Bonnie could barely see the action from where she was crouching, but it soon became clear that Grampa Banks must have forgotten to turn sideways before tackling the stairs.

Her grampa was now firmly wedged between two walls, legs dangling like wet spaghetti.

"Bonbon old man," came a muffled, apologetic voice, "I reckon I've made things worse."

Grampa Banks was stuck, and Anton Price looked like he was trying to turn into jelly and hide inside his own slippers. It was time Montgomery Bonbon took control of the situation. Staying low, squelching across the tea-soaked carpet like a soggy commando,

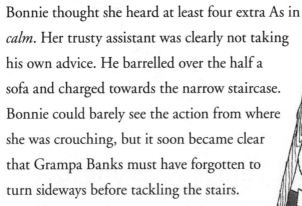

Bonnie shimmied her way over to the open window.

"Be careful!" begged Grampa Banks. "I can't see what you're doing, but please be careful!"

The large sash window was propped open with a wooden block. Bonnie reached a shaking hand up towards it. She could not stop herself from imagining a barrage of poison-tipped darts zipping in her direction. Nevertheless she kept stretching, walking her fingers up the wall like an acrobatic diplodocus, and over the windowsill where she could just … about … reach…

Finally she managed to get a finger and thumb around the splintery block. She pulled hard, making sure to keep her hand well clear of the frame. The wooden block tumbled onto the carpet. The sash window gave a warning rattle and then slid shut like a guillotine. *SHHHUNK!*

The instant the window was closed, Bonnie leaped to her feet. She looked out at Slender Lane for any sign of a villain vanishing with a blowpipe. The alley was empty. Several windows overlooked Anton's armchair, and Bonnie squinted at them one by one: horrible curtains … an angry Pekinese … a dead cactus … a sticker that came free with the *Bugle* that said: *Widdling Till I Die…*

Every window told a story, but which one had concealed the Blowpipe Killer?

"Can you see anything, Detective? Are we safe now?" asked Anton, who had almost managed to cringe his way under the coffee table.

"I believe the crisis, she has passed," said Bonnie, reluctant to turn away from the window in case the tiniest clue escaped her. "You are unhurt, Monsieur?" she asked over her shoulder.

"Yes … yes…" said Anton, wobbling to his feet. "Intact, you see. Intact, at least."

A very muted "Bravo, Bonbon!" came from the staircase. Grampa Banks would have to stay wedged in there for a little while longer. Bonnie was busy thinking.

It was clear that the killer had been aiming for Anton, but why? Were they targeting everyone who had witnessed the theft of the Widdlington Eagle? Bonnie frowned a sceptical frown. Rashida Zaki would have made a much better target when she was strolling around St Hilaria's churchyard in a rainbow blazer. It seemed more likely to Bonnie that the killer had struck because Anton Price had been about to reveal a vital clue to Montgomery Bonbon.

She dragged herself away from the window and helped the unsteady restorer onto his half a sofa.

"Please to continue, Monsieur Price. Explain to Bonbon your message most cryptic."

Anton took a breath and looked like he was about to change the subject again. Bonnie fixed him with a stare, projecting determination out of every strand of Montgomery Bonbon's moustache.

"You are safe now, Monsieur," said Bonnie, placing a reassuring hand on Anton's shoulder. "The killer, they wished to prevent you from telling to Bonbon your secret. I ask you to be a very brave boy, now."

Anton nodded. He took a large gulp of air, and began to speak.

"It's my boss, you see. Harriet Spruce. She is rather keen on plants. Absolutely potty about them, you might say. Perhaps you saw her…" Anton wiggled his fingers in an impression of the plants that grew out of Harriet's pockets.

Bonnie nodded. "*Ja*. It had not escaped the attention of Bonbon."

"Even I noticed," said the stairs.

Anton leaned towards Bonnie and spoke in a low voice. "I visited her at home, oh, several weeks ago now. She has quite a collection, you see. A very *expensive* array of specimens. It must cost an awful lot of money to buy such fabulous flowers. And, well, working in a museum is not particularly … remunerative." Anton's nervous fingers tugged at the loose threads in his old suit.

"Please to tell me: what is *remunerative*?" asked Bonnie. Another advantage of being a distinguished foreign gentleman is that it makes it very easy to ask what a funny word means.

"Forgive me, Detective. I mean to say that when it comes to pecuniary matters, the Hornville can be somewhat ... parsimonious."

"Please to tell me—" began Bonnie, but Grampa Banks interrupted from the stairs.

"He means the pay stinks!"

"Ah!" said Bonnie. "The pay at the museum, she stinks?"

"Well, yes. I suppose she does," said Anton with obvious discomfort. "But there's something else. I remembered Ms Spruce telling me that she had a cutting of something unusual in her hothouse. Something *poisonous*. I think she called it ... deadly frightshade."

"Deadly frightshade?" repeated Bonnie.

"I think she said it was a very rare exotic plant. And I believe it comes from—"

"South America," finished Bonnie with a sinking feeling.

"My goodness!" exclaimed Anton. "How *do* you do it, Detective?"

Bonnie and Grampa Banks sat in Bessie with all the windows rolled up tight. As far as she could tell, there was no sign that the Blowpipe Killer was still lurking in the vicinity, but Bonnie knew she would not relax properly until the culprit was caught.

"We'll have to tell Inspector Sands about the attack," she said.

"Oh, yes."

"But not just yet."

"Oh, no."

According to Anton, Harriet Spruce lived over in Widdlington on Seaview Road. Bonnie felt a sensation of sickly excitement at the prospect of tackling a bona fide suspect head-on.

"What are we waiting for? Let's go!"

Grampa Banks did not reply. He had been oddly quiet ever since she had had to clamber over him and pull him down the staircase of 11B Slender Lane. Instead he reached carefully into his jacket and pulled out a wooden picture frame. Bonnie recognized it immediately as one of Anton's old photographs.

"I must have picked this up by accident while I was wedged in the stairs. Something about it caught my eye. I thought to myself, this is the kind of thing our Bonnie would call a clue."

Taking pictures at crime scenes was one thing, but taking pictures from crime scenes? That was almost criminal. Bonnie was about to reprimand her assistant, but Grampa Banks interrupted her.

"Just have a look at it, love."

He placed the photograph in Bonnie's lap. It showed a dozen or so employees of the Hornville

Museum standing proudly in front of the entrance. Like all old photos, most of the faces looked stern and a little blurry. She recognized the man in the centre with the bushy beard and curly whiskers. Abelard Hornville, she thought.

She was correct. Underneath the photograph, the employees' names were written in thin calligraphic script. There was Abelard Hornville, alongside Eudora Potts, Maisie Potts, Gilbert Price...

"Don't you see it?" asked Grampa Banks, becoming a little impatient.

"See what?"

"Look at the date."

The date at the bottom of the frame read *1955*.

"And look at old Eudora Potts. Eh? See it?"

Bonnie worked back from the list of names and found Eudora Potts in the picture. There she was. A tall woman with her long hair tied back and her hands around…

"That's the—"

"Exactly." Grampa Banks grinned.

According to Bonnie's notes, the stolen eagle had been sold to the NJMFNOS in 1931. And yet, in this photograph, taken over two decades later, Eudora Potts was holding something that appeared for all the world to be the Widdlington Eagle.

"But that's impossible!" she protested.

"I know!"

Bonnie stared hard at the inexplicable picture, willing the people in it to come to life and explain everything.

"We'll have to tell the police that I … *borrowed* the photo, of course," said Grampa Banks.

"Oh, yes," agreed Bonnie.

"But not just yet?"

"Oh, no."

Bonnie paused for a moment, deep in thought.

"Can I have a lemon sherbet *now*?"

"I told you, they're all for me."

"Aw!"

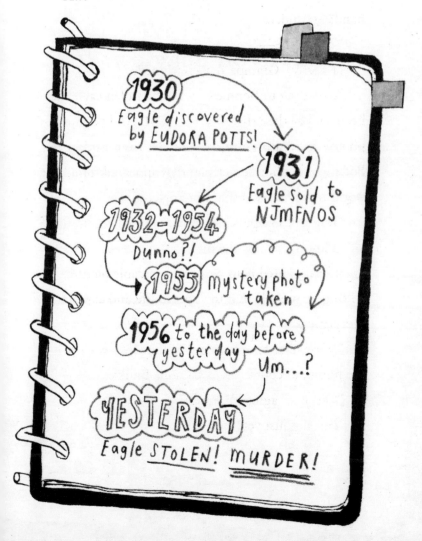

Chapter Seventeen

A Jungle on Seaview Road

Seaview Road was murderously steep, running up from
Widdlington's pebble beach and over Seaview Hill.
One misstep, one stumble, one trip, and you would be
tumbling all the way down and out to sea. You would
be in Copenhagen by the time anyone asked, "Where's
Janet?" (Assuming your name is Janet.)

Bonnie was puzzled by the name Seaview Road.
She could barely see the sea because of the weather-
beaten houses looming up out of the ground on either

side. They followed the road all the way over the hump of the hill, like spines on a dinosaur's back, blotting out the view. The stinging sea air whipped at Bonnie's face and salt began to crystallize in her false moustache as she and Grampa Banks approached number 135.

The poisoner's house?

Bonnie knew she had to tread carefully here, and not just to avoid ending up in Copenhagen.

"I used to sell ice cream up and down Seaview," wheezed Grampa Banks with his hands on his knees. "I always thought the motor would give out on the way up, and the brakes would give out on the way down! Odd folk round here. Bonkers for cranberry ice pops." Seeing Bonnie's expression, he trailed off. "Don't know if that's relevant to the case…"

Bonnie decided that total silence was the kindest way of letting Grampa Banks know that this information was *not* relevant to the case.

Nothing seemed to grow on Seaview Road. The tiny front yards were grey and sandy; there were no gardens – only pebbles, seashells and crazy paving that looked more sad than crazy.

That is, apart from house number 135, which looked like a slice of the Amazon had been dropped in the middle of Widdlington. The building stuck out like a piece of birthday cake on a bookshelf. Moss covered the low wall at the front and vines hung down from the guttering in great swags. Creepers clung to the peeling paintwork as if they were trying to pull the house down into the earth itself.

Bonnie stopped dead when she reached the front gate. The yard was thick with yellowish grass that came up to her shoulders. It looked razor sharp and, somehow, she knew it was full of things that buzzed and scuttled. She might even have been thinking about turning back, but one glance up at the roof changed her mind. Projecting out from it was a wrought-iron greenhouse. Its windows were steamed up, dripping with condensation; green leaves pressed wetly against the glass.

"The hothouse," Bonnie said to herself.

The plant known as deadly frightshade had to be lurking somewhere in there. Not far from Harriet Spruce and, perhaps, her blowpipe-wielding sidekick.

"The Usual Strategy?" Bonnie asked.

"You mean, I get clonked on the head and pass out, allowing the killer to escape?"

"No, the other Usual Strategy."

"I keep 'em talking while you pretend to go to the little detectives' room?"

"Exactly."

She pushed her way through the long grass. Bonnie Montgomery might be funny about creepy-crawlies, but Montgomery Bonbon was not. Bonnie let Grampa Banks ring the lichen-coated doorbell while she made sure her moustache was looking appropriately impressive.

It took Harriet Spruce a very long time to open the front door. She finally appeared wearing a lime-green housecoat with a camouflage body warmer on top – an outfit distinguished by being inappropriate both inside and out. In her hands she held a small potted sapling, the way a toddler might hold a teddy bear. Her frizzy hair was as much of a mess as her garden. It was the kind of hair, Bonnie noted, that might have benefitted from a hairpin.

"Fräulein Spruce," began Bonnie in Montgomery Bonbon's most bombastic tone. "A most delightful surprise!"

"But … this is my house," said Harriet.

"*Ja, ja,*" Bonnie scrambled, "for *you*! A most delightful surprise indeed! For you. I have one or two ever so very small questions to be asking. To you."

"Yes, of course," said Harriet, without seeming particularly delighted. "You're very welcome, Detective Bonbon. And of course, Mr…"

"Banks," supplied Grampa Banks, flashing her a smile she could not help returning. "Call me Clive."

Harriet absent-mindedly handed the sapling to Grampa Banks, who kept smiling but held it as if it were a poison-tipped dagger. Harriet led them inside, into the dark green interior of number 135.

Stepping across the threshold was like being plunged into an alien world. Huge rainforest plants lined the walls, and their great rubbery leaves formed an arch over Bonnie's head. Grampa Banks had to duck. The smell was intense – the mingled perfume of a hundred exotic flowers all at once. It reminded Bonnie of the high-street soap shop in Widdlington Old Town, the one that was so smelly it caused pedestrians to pass out in the street and wake up having bought forty quid's worth of vegan facial scrub.

They followed Harriet deeper inside as she weaved a winding path through the dense foliage. All around Bonnie, things seemed to slither and scurry. She shuddered at the sight of an enormous black caterpillar creeping its concertina creep underneath a blinking sunlamp. Bonnie clutched her raincoat tightly about her. She tried not to look at the glinting, iridescent eyes that seemed to sparkle out of dark corners. She tried not to imagine a blowpipe silently taking aim at the back of her neck.

No, Bonnie told herself firmly, a detective's job is to detect, not to jump to conclusions. Number 135 was certainly not the house of a normal person, but Bonnie was not sure she had ever met a completely normal person. Not being normal did not make someone a

murderer. *Evidence*. That was what Bonnie was here for.

Harriet ushered Bonnie and Grampa Banks into the sitting room and gestured towards a pair of comfy chairs that had shoots sprouting from the buttonholes. As the lady of the house stood in front of them with her hands clasped together, there was a rustling sound from the leaves overhead. Bonnie looked up, expecting to see a cat, and almost gasped as a scarlet macaw swooped down from some hidden perch and landed on Harriet's shoulder. The parrot wore a furious expression, and a little collar with a gold name tag.

"There you are, Hector! Say hello."

The bird fixed one beady marble eye on Bonnie, and stared intently. "Disguise," he croaked.

Even in the muggy jungle air, Bonnie felt herself go cold. Somehow the macaw had seen through Montgomery Bonbon's ensemble.

"Disguise!" screeched the macaw. "Disguise!"

Harriet chuckled a shrill chuckle.

"These guys? Why, it's the detective I told you about: Montgomery Bonbon, and his associate, Clive."

187

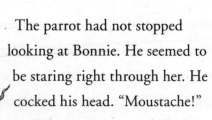

The parrot had not stopped looking at Bonnie. He seemed to be staring right through her. He cocked his head. "Moustache!"

"I know you must dash, but you can at least greet our guests."

"Moustache! Moustache!" screeched the macaw, flapping his wings in agitation and shedding red feathers on the carpet.

Red feathers, thought Bonnie. I've seen red feathers before.

"Oh, push off then, you old devil," Harriet scolded. "Go on, shoo!"

With an air of resentment and wounded dignity, the grizzled old macaw flapped lazily out of the sitting room. Bonnie realized she was holding her breath – and exhaled. She knew she needed to say something, but Montgomery Bonbon's usual wit and insight seemed to have flown out of the room along with that horrible parrot.

"I see you are liking the plants, Fräulein?" she said weakly.

"Not particularly," Harriet answered, brushing her hands lightly across thick, leathery leaves. "I never was especially keen. Someone gave me a Swiss cheese plant on my thirty-fifth birthday, and after that everyone else started giving me plants. Then I started buying plants. I don't know... After a while, there's nothing you can do – you're the plant lady."

Bonnie found herself absent-mindedly squeezing the flowery hairgrip in her raincoat pocket. She could not ask Harriet about it yet. If the museum's manager *was* guilty, the last thing Bonnie wanted to do was alert her. She hesitated just a moment too long and Grampa Banks jumped in to rescue her by asking a question about a large yellow flower. It turned out to be an American skunk cabbage.

This was why the Usual Strategy was so effective. Her mum often said that Grampa Banks was very good at speaking to "women of a certain age". Bonnie did not understand why Liz was so vague about what that age actually was; it was supposed to be certain, after all. But whatever age it was, Harriet was certainly a woman of it. She seemed very happy speaking to Grampa Banks, and she hardly noticed when Montgomery Bonbon asked to make use of the facilities.

"The toilet is on the first-floor landing. The door doesn't lock, and you'll have to step around the mushrooms," she said, gesturing vaguely in the direction of the stairs.

Bonnie left Grampa Banks and Harriet chuckling together in the sitting room. She hoped her grandfather was simply being charming and had not forgotten that Harriet was currently their chief suspect. But she did not have time to worry about that – she had a poisonous plant to find.

She squelched and creaked her way up the uneven staircase, dodging mosquitoes and ducking under drooping tendrils. As she passed the toilet door, she made sure to open and close it loudly, just in case Harriet was listening downstairs.

She had to creep up another flight of stairs before she saw the hatch into the attic. The ceiling around it was covered in black mould and home to a family of snails. The hatch was slightly ajar – Harriet must have

been working up in the hothouse when they rang the
doorbell. There was a small metal ring screwed into
the hatch, which meant there had to be a long pole
with a hook on the end somewhere near by. Bonnie
looked around, fingers twitching impatiently. There it
was, in a somewhat deforested corner of the landing.

Bonnie grabbed the pole with both hands and
tried desperately to get the hook into the ring hanging
down from the hatch. She had never felt smaller. She
kept swinging the pole – *whiff, whiff, whiff* – past the
ring on the hatch, like an upside-down golfer missing
the ball. She tightened her grip on the very bottom of
the pole and stretched her arms up as far as she
could. She could hear her shoes creaking,
her raincoat straining. She could feel
the sweat beading on her upper lip.

Whiff, whiff, whiff… Click!

Bonnie pulled down on the pole
with all her strength, tumbling over as
the hatch swung open and a folding
ladder clattered noisily down onto the
landing. The surrounding insects stopped

191

chirping for a moment as if to say, "You're in trouble now."

Kneeling on the landing carpet, Bonnie poked her nose through the banisters and peered down the staircase. She waited for the pad of Harriet's slippered footsteps on the stairs, but it did not come. Instead she heard the sound of distant chatter and Harriet asking, "How do you take your tea?" Grampa Banks must have made his "In a cup, please!" joke, because Harriet let out another peal of laughter.

This would be Grampa Banks's seventh cup of the day. But Bonnie was not too worried – it was remarkably hard to separate detective work from tea drinking. And seven cups was well below his usual twelve.

She pulled herself upright on the ivy-coiled banister rail. She looked up into the haze of Harriet's rooftop greenhouse, then began her climb into the hothouse.

Who Killed Oliver Munday?
Suspects
Herman Hornville -
weird daughter?
weird Dana
Anton Price -
How old is this guy?
Harriet Spruce -
What's wi all the
plant
Rashida Za
Something
about he
her som
Old enough to know Harriet's Secret!
Anton
dart

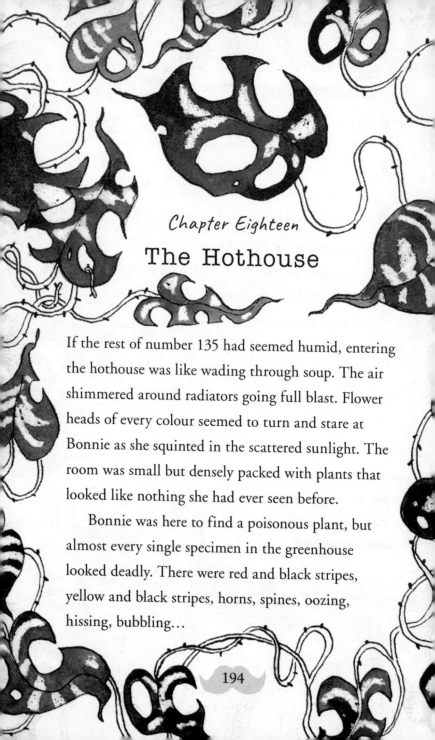

Chapter Eighteen

The Hothouse

If the rest of number 135 had seemed humid, entering the hothouse was like wading through soup. The air shimmered around radiators going full blast. Flower heads of every colour seemed to turn and stare at Bonnie as she squinted in the scattered sunlight. The room was small but densely packed with plants that looked like nothing she had ever seen before.

Bonnie was here to find a poisonous plant, but almost every single specimen in the greenhouse looked deadly. There were red and black stripes, yellow and black stripes, horns, spines, oozing, hissing, bubbling…

Her whole body prickled with heat, and she felt as if she could hear the creak of the plants growing, straining against the panes. It was like being a clue under her own magnifying glass, frazzling in the beams of the scorching Widdlington sun.

Not daring to touch anything, Bonnie crouched down and squinted at the plant pots. She was hoping to see cute labels or adorable wooden signs with the plants' names. She found nothing. All she ended up with was a terrible woozy sensation when she stood back up. It was like her head had been swapped for a hot-air balloon. She steadied herself on a small workbench and wiped the perspiration from her face.

A sick feeling crept up from the pit of her stomach. She reached up again and carefully touched her upper lip. She was not wearing Montgomery Bonbon's moustache. It must have fallen off at some point since she left the sitting room.

Was coming here a mistake?

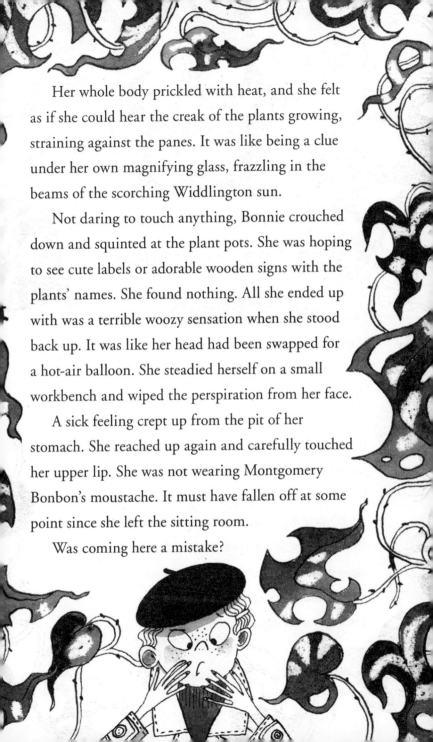

She fanned herself with one of Harriet's botanical field guides.

Blundering into the hothouse without a proper plan? Losing my moustache? Imbecile!

She felt her cheeks flush; the breeze from *Culpeper's Compendium of Poisonous Plants* was doing very little to help.

What was she thinking? As if the vital clue was just going to appear right under her nose!

She might as well have expected to find the answer in:

Bonnie stared at the book in her hands. She had grabbed it because it had stood out from all the other books on Harriet's workbench. Unlike those blotchy, drab and ancient volumes, it was pristine.

Bonnie's moustache-less face was reflected back at her from its glossy dust jacket. With unsteady fingers, she riffled through the colourful pages of beautiful but poisonous plants: angel's trumpet … bleeding heart … cowbane…

She found deadly frightshade – and almost slammed the book shut. From downstairs, she heard the piercing whistle of the kettle boiling.

A glance at the illustration had told Bonnie that she was standing extremely close to the deadly frightshade plant itself. In fact, its drooping leaves and purple flowers were almost touching Montgomery Bonbon's old raincoat. But that was not what had alarmed her. She opened the book again with trembling fingers to double-check.

FRIGHTSHADE, Deadly

Common names: griefwort, devil's hood, bitter Jack, nasty Geoff

Deadly frightshade is a flowering perennial, native to South America and parts of east Yorkshire. It grows three to four feet tall, producing hooded purple flowers from a fleshy grey-white stem.

Her eyes skimmed down the paragraph.

A lethal, fast-acting poison can be extracted by boiling the petals in water…

Boiling the petals in water. Bonnie snapped the book shut again. What had she been thinking? She had been so determined to find Harriet's deadly frightshade that she had left Grampa Banks taking tea with a poisoner!

She clattered back down the ladder with *Culpeper's Compendium* under her arm. There, on the banister rail, was Hector the scarlet macaw, holding Montgomery Bonbon's famous moustache in his hooked beak. Scarlet macaws do not have the muscles required to raise an eyebrow sarcastically, but clearly no one had told Hector that. He seemed to take a moment to enjoy Bonnie's reaction and then flew off down the stairs.

Bonnie tumbled after him. Seconds later, she was outside the sitting room – breathless and peering through a crack in the door. Hector was perched on a low branch, still wearing the moustache and smugly waiting to be noticed. Harriet was lifting a teapot off a tray, and Grampa Banks was smiling, obliviously, in his chair.

Montgomery Bonbon would normally have burst through the door, moustache abristle, thrown *Culpeper's Compendium* down on the coffee table and shouted, *"J'accuse!"* But Montgomery Bonbon's moustache was already in the room, and without it Bonnie was just a ten-year-old child wearing an oversized raincoat and a fetching beret.

Harriet Spruce was now pouring tea into a substantial-looking mug; Bonnie needed to act fast. If rescuing Grampa Banks meant revealing her identity and sacrificing her career as the world's greatest detective, then that was what she had to do. She took a deep breath, drew back her shoulders — and reached for the sitting-room door handle.

Except, sitting on the door handle was a velvety black shape: a huge furry caterpillar, rippling patiently millimetres from Bonnie's fingers. Bonnie had never deliberately touched a creepy-crawly before, but Grampa Banks's mug was already gliding towards his lips. There was no time to hesitate. She grabbed the caterpillar, planted it on her face, and flung the door open.

It may surprise you to learn that the caterpillar clinging to Bonnie's top lip had no previous acting experience. In fact, it had no formal training in the performing arts at all. But Montgomery Bonbon's moustache was the role it was hatched to play.

"*J'affuse!*" Bonnie cried, having underestimated quite how furry the caterpillar was.

Grampa Banks clinked his mug hurriedly down onto Harriet's tea tray. With a dramatic flourish, Bonnie opened *Culpeper's Compendium* so wide she heard the spine crack.

"You murffered Oliver Munffay with the ffoison of the deadly ffrightshade fflant!"

Harriet looked down at the illustration of the deadly frightshade, and then up at Bonnie with an expression of confusion and horror.

She burst into tears.

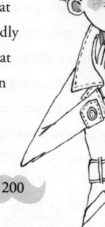

A blue police light flashed through the window, illuminating the foliage like lightning in a tropical storm. In all the commotion, Bonnie had managed to wrestle her false moustache back from Hector. Now the haughty macaw was being interrogated by Inspector Sands, whose hair had never looked frizzier than in the humidity of Harriet's home.

"SQUAWK! Wanna cracker?"

"Are you trying to bribe an officer of the law?"

"Who's a pretty boy?"

"I'll ask the questions, sunshine."

Grampa Banks was trying to help Constable Simon put handcuffs on the deadly frightshade, which had been brought carefully down from the hothouse into the sitting room. There was every reason to suspect this would go on for a while, since between them they had somehow managed to handcuff Simon to an occasional table.

Bonnie was not feeling the buzz that usually came with solving a case. Harriet's house was overfull of things that buzzed. Perhaps that was the problem.

She made her way out of the stifling jungle house

and onto Seaview Road, where a welcome evening breeze was blowing. Harriet was sitting in the back of a police car parked crookedly in front of the house. She had not been allowed to take any of her plants, and she slumped in the seat dejectedly, like a dead leaf waiting to be swept away.

Maybe that was why Bonnie's buzz did not feel very buzzy. No perpetrator Bonnie had apprehended before had looked so very sad. When you caught them, criminals were supposed to say something like, "Very clever, you revolting little man!" before leaping off the top of a clock tower down a zip line. They were usually furious and spitting feathers! (Quite literally in the case of the Dodderingham Ostrich Biter.)

They were not supposed to start *blubbing*.

Harriet caught sight of Bonnie as she passed the police car.

"It wasn't me, I swear," sobbed Harriet as the constable behind the wheel revved the car into life. "I would never... I could never... I don't know the first thing about blowpipes! I only just bought that book. Please!"

Bonnie watched Harriet Spruce disappear, her palm pressed against the window, down a darkening Seaview Road. Bonnie was almost relieved. She had never found it difficult to look a suspect in the face before.

Wait! The hairpin!

Bonnie whipped the hairpin out of her pocket, but it was too late. She had been so focused on finding the deadly frightshade plant that she had forgotten to ask Harriet about the hairpin. Still, perhaps she would have a chance to compare it with—

"So! It was *you*!"

Before Bonnie could turn round, Inspector Sands had swooped down from behind her and snatched the hairpin from her fingers.

"I should have known, Bonbon. Trying to slow me down, eh?"

With a fluid motion, Inspector Sands swept her hair back into a perfectly spherical bun and deftly clipped it in place with the hairpin.

"The… The hairpin…" Bonnie felt dazed. "It is yours, Inspecteur?"

"*Pff!* As if you didn't know!" scoffed Inspector Sands.

"But … the flower design—"

"Just because I am a successful female role model in this community," said Inspector Sands, "doesn't mean I don't enjoy a shiny, flowery little whatnot. Move with the times, Bonbon. It's the twenty-first century."

Inspector Sands clomped off with an air of triumph. "That's two mysteries solved. Not bad. Not bad at all," she congratulated herself.

Bonnie tottered across the deserted Seaview Road and sat down on the opposite kerb. She had never had any evidence that the hairpin belonged to Harriet. She had let herself get carried away. Sands must have dropped it near the fire escape after Bonnie was shooed out of the museum. That explained why the inspector's hair had grown so wild.

Montgomery Bonbon should have seen it.

And there was another thing. A little itch at the back of Bonnie's brain ever since she had been in the hothouse.

"It did look new…" she murmured. She was not speaking in Montgomery Bonbon's voice. She did not feel like it right now.

"What do you mean, love?" asked Grampa Banks, lowering himself onto the kerb beside her.

"The book I found, the one with the deadly frightshade recipe… It looked brand new. It even smelled new, once I opened it downstairs. What if…" Bonnie took a deep breath. "What if Harriet is actually innocent?"

Grampa Banks took hold of Bonnie's hand and gave it a squeeze. "I was about your age when I did this for the first time."

"Did what?"

"Made a mistake that hurt someone."

Though it gave her a horrible sinking feeling inside, Bonnie knew that Grampa Banks was right. She had felt so confident when she accused Harriet Spruce of being the murderer. She had been so very certain that she was right. But something did not fit. There were too many loose ends. The case was not solved.

The great Montgomery Bonbon had failed.

FRIGHTSHADE, Deadly

Common names: griefwort, devil's hood, bitter Jack, nasty Geoff

Deadly frightshade is a flowering perennial, native to South America and parts of east Yorkshire. It grows three to four feet tall, producing hooded purple flowers from a fleshy grey-white stem. Gardeners be warned: the deadly frightshade is highly toxic and even the sight of its purple colouring has been known to induce nausea in children and small dogs. A lethal, fast-acting poison can be extracted by boiling the petals in water. So, for goodness' sake, do not do that.

HE TAB (CO

POSSESSION OF

SPEAKING TO

IS MOVING

ATTEMPTED

BRINGING

'FIVE ITE

TRESPA

- UNAUTHORIZED SURVE
- CLIMBING THROUGH THE KITCHEN HATCH TO GRAMPA BANK'S ROOM
- BADGERING A WITNESS
- BADGERING A BADGER
- IMPERSONATING A VENTRILOQUIST
- SNEAKING OUT AFTER TEATIME
- ARRESTING AN INNOCENT WOMAN?

Chapter Nineteen
The Doldrums

Gloom settled on Bonnie like a heavy winter blanket. She had been lying on the kitchen floor tiles, arms and legs splayed like a starfish, for almost an hour now. On the table, today's *Widdler* screamed:
KILLER CAUGHT: SANDS DOES IT AGAIN.

The more Bonnie thought about it, the more it seemed clear that Harriet Spruce was not a murderer. It was true that Harriet had access to the rare and deadly poison that killed Oliver. But she had been on the other side of the turret-room door with two witnesses when the dart was fired. And what was she supposed to have done with the Widdlington Eagle?

Bonnie was certain that Inspector Sands did not have the answers. It felt to Bonnie like all the clues had been put together in the wrong order, like one of Abelard Hornville's horrible glassy-eyed monsters.

Bonnie raised her arms and legs in the air, stuck them out perfectly straight, dead-fly style, then let them flop back down onto the floor with a loud *slap-slap-slap-slap*. She sighed. She had been hoping that would jolt her brain cells into action, but she was no better off than before. She felt like a fraud. If she could not solve a locked-room mystery, was she worthy to wear Montgomery Bonbon's moustache?

There was no doubt about it: Bonnie was in the Doldrums.

The Doldrums affect all great detectives. One minute you can be catching a cat burglar, outfoxing a forger or busting a blackmailer and the next you will be swooning on a sofa, unable to solve the word search on the back of your choccy rice flakes. Every time Bonnie tried to concentrate her mind on a detail in the case, it seemed to drift away from her, like a bad dream where the ground keeps crumbling beneath your feet.

Grampa Banks had worked on enough cases with Bonnie to know all about the Doldrums.

"Would you like to sit up here with me, love?" he asked from a seat at the table. "I can make us some peppermint tea. We don't have to talk about the case."

"Prprprprpr," said floor Bonnie.

"Come on, I'm gasping here. I haven't had a cuppa since breakfast."

Bonnie could tell she was being manipulated; it was only 9.45 a.m. But with a drawn-out *"Euuuugh!"* she managed to drag herself off the floor, arms swinging like pendulums, and slump grumpily down into the wooden chair opposite Grampa Banks.

She glared at the front of *The Widdler*. Grampa

Banks quickly flipped it over to the sports section, which yelled: *Local Favourite Disappoints*. Bonnie groaned again and Grampa Banks hurriedly flipped to a different page.

Bonbon Made Me Sick! Sweet Shop Scandal.

He flipped again.

FOOTWEAR REVIEWS: Thick Gumshoe Proves Useless.

He flipped and flipped and flipped.

FAILURE! LOSER! FAKE!

"Just put it away, please," croaked Bonnie, flopping forward onto the table.

Grampa Banks crumpled up *The Widdler* and shuffled over to the kettle, where he dropped the paper unceremoniously into the recycling bin. He boiled the kettle, filled the teapot and poured out two big cups. And then he sat with Bonnie, waiting quietly for their peppermint teas to cool.

Bonnie usually drank peppermint tea when she needed a flash of inspiration. But inspiration can strike in many different ways. When the mathematician Isaac Newton was bonked on the head by a falling apple, he was inspired to buy a hat. When the philosopher Archimedes stepped into his bath and sloshed water over the sides, the people downstairs were inspired to find a new flat. Whether inspiration is dropping off a tree or dripping through your ceiling, you never know when it is about to strike.

Bonnie did not realize that inspiration was travelling towards her at this moment, and it looked exactly like Liz Montgomery.

"How's my girl?" she asked, draping her arms around Bonnie like an enormous soft scarf.

"Mmmf," replied Bonnie.

Bonnie could sense Grampa Banks mouthing, "Doldrums!" as though it were an embarrassing bottom problem you did not want to say out loud.

"Oh! Are you being a sulky-pops, my love?" asked Bonnie's mum, planting a kiss on the crown of her daughter's head.

Sulky-pops, thought Bonnie. Sulky. Pops. Sherlock Holmes never got called a sulky-pops. Or, if he did, he definitely did not let Watson put it in the books.

"What's the matter? Can I help?" asked her mum, sliding into the chair next to Bonnie. Bonnie did not enjoy lying to her mum, but frequently she had no choice.

"No, I'm just stuck … on a puzzle."

"Aw, sweetheart. You know what might help?"

"What?" asked Bonnie sceptically. She recognized the look in her mum's eyes. Liz was about to suggest dancing naked on the full moon or a raw cabbage detox.

"Well … a friend of mine says—"

"Is it Guru Jonathan Jonathan?"

"A *friend of mine* says that when you're all tied up in knots, what you need to do is meditate."

"No way. No. Uh-uh."

"Come on, you said you'd give it a try."

"When?" demanded Bonnie.

"The other day! You said, 'Absolutely. One hundred per cent.'"

Bonnie had a nasty feeling she actually *had* said that back in Chapter 5. "Yeah, but—"

"Shush, shush, shush! Give it a try. Close your eyes for me."

Arguing with Liz was like trying to escape from the affections of an Old English sheepdog. Eventually you just had to give in and let it jump all over you.

"OK, OK. My eyes are closed," grumbled Bonnie.

"No, they're not," chorused Grampa Banks and Bonnie's mum at the same time.

"All right, they are now!"

Bonnie scrunched her eyes closed and listened to the sound of her mum's voice.

"OK, now take a deep breath. Hold it. Now, Guru J— *My friend*, whoever they may be, says that when you have a problem, it can help to look at it from a different perspective. Try opening your third eye."

"I only have *two eyes*," grunted Bonnie.

"Less talking, more relaxing!" snapped her mum, before transitioning back into her soothing meditation voice. "Now breathe out … and iiiin … and out … and iiiin…"

Bonnie breathed. Out and in. Out and in.

Annoyingly she began to feel a little bit better. Her arms were pleasantly floppy, and she no longer felt like a weight was pressing down on her. Probably the peppermint tea, she told herself.

"Now, your third eye is right here." Bonnie's mum tapped her very gently on the middle of the forehead. "And when you learn to open it, you unlock your…" She paused dramatically. "Powers of perception."

"You don't really believe this stuff, do you?" asked Grampa Banks under his breath.

"None of your business whether I do or don't," hissed Liz.

Whatever her mum thought, Bonnie did not believe in psychic abilities. Even if they were real, detectives were certainly not allowed to use them. It was not fair to have a detective who could read minds and see through walls. The criminals would not stand a chance. And if detectives could predict the future, they could stop murders from happening in the first place. It would ruin all the fun.

Afterwards, Bonnie was not certain how long she

had spent breathing in and out, in and out. But with her eyes closed, her mother's voice in her ears and the vapours of peppermint tea tickling her nostrils, something started to happen. Like the twinkling of a star, or the tinkling of a distant bell, an idea began to form in her mind.

Psychic abilities, she thought. Hold on a moment…

The twinkling star got brighter.

Someone's story doesn't make sense…

The tinkling bell drifted closer.

One of my suspects would have to be psychic…

And closer and brighter.

So that means…

"Yes!" cried Bonnie.

"Blorb!" spluttered Grampa Banks, sploshing peppermint tea onto the table. He must have nodded off while Bonnie was boarding the astral plane.

"What happened; what's the matter?" asked Bonnie's mum in alarm.

"Nothing's the matter. Nothing at all. Meditating worked!" said Bonnie, hopping off her chair. "I've just had a eureka moment."

"Please don't tell me you've flooded the bathroom again," said Liz. "I don't care what those Ancient Greeks got up to—"

"No! The bathroom's fine. I think I know how to solve my ... puzzle. Thank you, Mum!"

"But according to Guru Jonathan Jo—"

Bonnie cut her mum off with a hug. "I didn't need Guru Jonathan Jonathan's help – I just needed *you*."

Bonnie had met someone who seemed to possess psychic abilities. That person was the museum's owner, Herman Hornville. She thought back to what Dana had told her in the church: her father had telephoned the police from their flat, and then they left to visit the museum. Everyone knew there were no CCTV cameras in the museum. *So how did Herman Hornville know what had happened before he got there?*

Two possibilities leaped out at Bonnie. The first was that Herman Hornville had planned the whole crime himself. The second was that Mr Hornville had some secret way of seeing into the museum when he was not there. Could Dana's father have a third eye of his own ... and a fourth eye, and a fifth eye, and a sixth eye? The idea made Bonnie's detective instincts prickle. From the moment she had entered the museum, she had felt like Hornville's Monsters were watching her.

What if she was right? What if they actually were?

She remembered the eerie stare of the monsters' glass eyes with a shiver. If her gut was right, that was where Mr Hornville had hidden several secret security cameras. And those cameras might just have recorded the killer escaping with the Widdlington Eagle. This could be the break Bonnie needed to solve the case.

In the blink of a squirrelephant's eye, Bonnie was sitting in Bessie's passenger seat. She had a fresh hunch, and a detective with a hunch can do only one thing: snoop. She needed to get inside Herman Hornville's flat, yet even the great Montgomery Bonbon would struggle to barge into the museum owner's home without an invitation.

Bonnie pulled Dana's crumpled card out of her pocket and tried to smooth it out with her thumbs. She remembered Dana's words: "Just drop by if you feel like it. Find out more about the choir or whatever."

Or whatever, thought Bonnie, as Grampa Banks sat down in the driver's seat next to her.

"Where to, guv?" he asked.

"Museum Street, please," replied Bonnie with steely determination.

"You know, while you were meditating there, love, I had a bit of…"

"A nap?"

Grampa Banks grinned. "Well, yes. But I was actually going to say … inspiration of my own."

"You'd better tell me on the way."

A Study in Scarlet by Sir Arthur Conan Doyle

Holmes was certainly not a difficult man to live with… Nothing could exceed his energy when the working fit was upon him; but now and again a reaction would seize him, and for days on end he would lie upon the sofa in the sitting room, hardly uttering a word or moving a muscle from morning to night. Had he been any other man than my friend Sherlock Holmes, I would have accounted him a right sulky-pops.

Chapter Twenty
Dana's Plan

Bonnie was waiting for the lift in the lobby of 142 Museum Street.

The lobby was a grand, high-ceilinged space where everything seemed to sparkle. Crystal chandeliers shimmered over Bonnie's head. Under her feet was a floor of polished marble, and in front of her, the lift's brass filigree gleamed enchantingly.

Bonnie tried to imagine what it would be like to live here. Her house did not even have a lobby, never mind one with whatever filigree was. Everywhere she looked there were more statues of people who had forgotten how to wear clothes properly. This place was swanky.

The lift pinged, and the brushed-metal doors slid open without a sound. Bonnie was surprised to see a little grey man sitting in the corner wearing a bellboy's hat.

"Where to, miss?" asked the man.

For someone who was used to being addressed as "Monsieur" or "Detective" while solving a case, Bonnie was almost startled by "miss". She glanced nervously at the card in her hand:

Dana Hornville Esq.
CHORAL SINGER, GRADE 7
PIANIST & COMPETITIVE ARCHER
Flat 3, 142 Museum Street,
Widdlington Old Town

"Um… Flat three. Please."

Bonnie realized the man was waiting for her to step inside, and she bustled into the mirrored lift. She hesitated. She was always happy to let Grampa Banks ring a doorbell, but she felt a bit weird about a strange man pressing the lift button for her.

Maybe I should just press it, she thought, raising her finger. But the man gave her a look that seemed to say, "*No!* If the residents of this building realized that they could press the lift buttons themselves, I would be out of a job in two seconds. Destitute! Outcast! A discarded banana peel on the rubbish heap of life! Is that what you want?"

Bonnie did not want the man to become a banana peel, so she quickly put her button-finger away. He pressed the button with a large number three on it.

"Nice work," said Bonnie, and the little grey man smiled a little grey smile. With a gentle hiss, the lift travelled upwards, so swiftly and smoothly that Bonnie barely knew she had left the ground.

"Flat three," croaked the man as the doors opened to reveal another marble-lined lobby. There was a set of heavy double doors in front of Bonnie, with a pull cord on the right-hand side.

She pulled on the cord, and a muted *ding-dong* rang out.

Bonnie could sense the man watching to see if she would be welcomed inside or told to get lost.

Suddenly she realized that there actually was a good chance she would be turned away. What if Dana was not in? What if she had changed her mind? Maybe Bonnie should have come dressed as Montgomery Bonbon after all.

She found herself staring at Dana's business card again. She compared it with the business card she had created for herself:

Bonnie Montgomery
Esq.
child + potential
Friend

The whole scheme was a mistake. But it was too late to back out now. Bonnie could hear a *clack-clack-clack* coming from the other side of the closed doors. She knew immediately that it was the sound of Herman Hornville's shoes rapping on the marble floor as he approached the entrance.

The doors swung open. Herman Hornville stood, framed in the doorway, like the life-size portrait that hung on the wall of the Hornville Museum. Somehow his triangular beard looked even pointer than it had the first time Bonnie had seen him.

"Yes?" Mr Hornville said, in a way that made it sound like the most demanding and intimidating word in the dictionary.

"Um … Bonnie Montgomery," she said, holding out her embarrassing business card. "Is … is Dana in?"

Mr Hornville snapped the card out of Bonnie's hand and squinted at it very closely. Bonnie wondered for a moment if he was going to snaffle it down and eat it. Instead he smiled politely and said, "Come in, Miss Montgomery."

The great doors closed behind Bonnie with a muted *shhhhupf.* She had been expecting the inside to be like the Hornville Museum: cluttered with dusty old antiques. But it was much more like Herman Hornville himself: clean, angular and severe. Bonnie could imagine searching all day without turning up a single speck of dust in the whole place.

"Dana," called Mr Hornville in a voice that was not particularly loud but bounced off all the polished surfaces in his home. "You have a visitor."

"Bonnie," cried Dana, appearing from a doorway and immediately grabbing Bonnie by the arm. "You came!"

Dana virtually dragged Bonnie through the Hornvilles' spotless apartment, swung her into her bedroom and slammed the door.

"Don't slam the door, Dana," came her father's muffled voice, followed by the retreating *clack-clack-clack* of his footsteps. "I shall be in my study," he called out. "Don't forget about this afternoon."

Dana's room was a little different from the rest of the apartment. Bonnie felt like she had opened a haunted doll's house and peered inside. The dark purple wallpaper was patterned with interlocking thorns and the four-poster bed had its own roof. A wicker chair was creaking under the weight of old teddies so threadbare they looked like little zombies.

The girls flopped onto the bed and Dana drew the embroidered drapes around them, like the walls of a cosy fortress. Bonnie felt instantly at home. This was the room of someone who appreciated mystery.

But, however comfortable they were, Bonnie could

not allow plush bedclothes to distract her from her mission. She was here on a case. She needed to muster her inner resolve. She needed to apply the knowledge she had gained as Montgomery Bonbon. She needed – oh, so skilfully – to steer the conversation towards Herman Hornville's secret.

A few minutes later, they were talking about cheese.

"So, I'm going to a cheese tasting this afternoon," said Dana, rolling her eyes in a way that implied she would rather go to a bottom-kicking festival.

"What's a cheese tasting?" asked Bonnie, feeling a keen twinge of embarrassment for not knowing.

"Apparently it's where you taste all different kinds of cheese."

Bonnie thought for a moment. "So what's the difference between cheese tasting and cheese *eating*?"

"Um… Well, Father sometimes does wine tastings. If it's anything like that, they'll just chew the cheese and then spit it out."

"Ugh!" said Bonnie, pulling a face. "Who wants to be in a room full of people spitting cheese all over the place?"

"I imagine they have … a bucket," said Dana, starting to grin.

"Ew! A stinky chewed-up cheese bucket?"

Bonnie enjoyed making Dana laugh again. The way the Hornville girl talked made her seem so much older and wiser than Bonnie. But when she laughed a stupid, happy, snorting laugh, it made Bonnie want to laugh too.

"Oh yeees, Reginald," said Bonnie, putting on her best rich-person voice, "parse me mine spit bucket, good fellow! This cheese is magnificent. *Pthoough*!"

Dana laughed. "Urgh! I shall be sick!"

"Well, then it's good they have a bucket."

"Euurgh!"

Dana hugged her knees, rocking back on the bed, still laughing. Bonnie did the same, rolling over onto one of Dana's tasselled pillows.

The pillow crinkled.

In Bonnie's experience, pillows tended not to crinkle. They *floomphed*, certainly, but they did not crinkle. Perhaps rich-people pillows *did* crinkle?

For all Bonnie knew, fancy pillows were filled with crisps in case you fancied a late-night snack, but she doubted it. She reached under the pillow, seeking the source of the sound.

"Ah," said Dana, suddenly serious, sitting upright and adjusting her glasses.

Bonnie pulled out a copy of today's *Widdler*. She was getting sick of the sight of that newspaper.

"I was reading about the murder when you rang the doorbell," said Dana guiltily.

"Please don't tell Father."

"I won't," promised Bonnie, who was looking at a caricature of Montgomery Bonbon next to a drawing of a chocolate teapot. The caption read: *Spot the Difference!*

"Father doesn't like me reading it. 'Hornvilles do not take *The Widdler*,'" said Dana, imitating her father's voice. "'It is tabloidesque.'"

Tabloidesque was a brilliant, grown-up sounding word. Bonnie made a mental note to use it, and also to find out what it meant. Hopefully not in that order.

"Plus, I think he's cross that I followed him to the museum on the night of the … the murder. He doesn't want me involved."

Bonnie tried to look cool. She even remembered to inspect her fingernails.

"*Are* you involved?"

"No!" said Dana emphatically. "But…"

Bonnie looked at Dana over the top of the newspaper. Now would have been the perfect moment to wobble her moustache.

"No, I wasn't involved, but…" Dana hesitated again. "Do you remember, you told me you were at the museum when it happened?"

"Yes," said Bonnie carefully, "I was there with my grampa."

"There's something I don't understand. Did I tell you that my father called the police from here in the flat? Well, he did, and" – Dana's voice grew very quiet – "I can't help asking myself… *How did he know what had happened?*"

Bonnie was stunned. She blinked her eyes. If she had known how to blink her ears, she would have done so too.

"You probably think I'm completely potty," said Dana, "but I believe my father has a hidden camera that lets him keep an eye on everything that happens in the museum."

Blink, blink.

"Don't you get it? The camera might have seen who killed Ollie!"

Blink.

"Bonnie!"

"That's a-a-a," Bonnie stammered, "a very interesting idea…"

"So you'll help me? I didn't know if I could ask you."

"Help you what?"

Dana took Bonnie's hand and leaned closer. "Help me sneak into my father's study."

Chapter Twenty-One

Hornville's Secret

"Here's the plan," whispered Dana.

They stood outside the imposing door to Herman Hornville's private sanctuary. It was made of dark polished wood with strips of inlaid brass. Bonnie had never seen a less approachable door. Just when she had started to get the hang of talking to Dana, she was once again tripping over her words and sweating behind her ears. Bonnie hadn't even known you *could* sweat behind your ears.

"I'll knock on the door and create a distraction. I'm good at distractions…"

On the one hand, Bonnie felt guilty for not being honest with Dana. On the other hand, the Hornville girl seemed to have everything worked out. Was this how Grampa Banks felt when Bonnie dragged him all over town on a case?

"Then you sneak inside and snoop around. Got it?" asked Dana.

"M-maybe *I* should distract him, and you go inside?"

Bonnie felt like a traitor to Montgomery Bonbon just for suggesting it, but she did not want to admit to Dana that she found her father more than a little frightening. The idea of hearing him come up behind her making that clack-clack-clack noise made her shiver.

"I've been trying to get in there ever since I learned to walk, honestly. I'm forbidden, prohibited, banned … but you're not," said Dana devilishly.

"I don't think—"

"Anyway, Father won't talk to you for more than two minutes. Children bore him." She paused. "I mean, *other* children. Now quickly, hide behind that Laflamme." Dana gestured towards several heavy-looking sculptures on marble plinths.

"Behind the *what*?"

"The Laflamme!"

Bonnie hid behind the ugliest of the sculptures and Dana raised her hand to knock on the study door.

"Wait!" said Bonnie. "What if he comes back while I'm in there?"

"Then I'll … give you a signal. I'll say 'cock-a-doodle-doo!'"

"Cock-a-doodle-doo?"

"Yes, now hide!"

Dana knocked on the door. Bonnie flinched down behind the marble plinth as the door swished opened and Mr Hornville loomed out.

Bonnie did not even listen to the story Dana invented as she led her father away from his study and into their brightly lit living room. She knew Dana's ruse would be as brilliant and daring as everything Dana seemed to do. Bonnie's eyes were fixed on the door, and her mind was focused on the case. As Herman Hornville disappeared round a corner, the door to his office was still closing – slowly, noiselessly. Bonnie darted across the marble and slipped through the gap.

She was in.

The inside of Mr Hornville's study was as scrupulously clean as the rest of his apartment. One wall was lined with books and the other with picture frames. Bonnie recognized the bearded face of Abelard Hornville frowning down at her fuzzily from an old photograph. And there was Eudora Potts, at work with a lump of clay, alongside a dozen other monochrome museum employees.

Mr Hornville's grand mahogany desk sat beneath a large window and Bonnie found it alarming. It did not look like any desk she had seen before. There was no stack of old, unwashed teacups. There were no pens, no paper, no computer. The dark surface was so clean it looked to Bonnie like it had popped straight out of a catalogue. But the sight of the desk itself was not what alarmed Bonnie. What bothered her was what she was not seeing.

She had expected to find something in here that would prove she was right. She was looking for Herman Hornville's third eye. But there was no sign of it.

Clack.

There were no monitors, no screens of any kind.

Clack.

And if Mr Hornville did not have a secret window into the museum, there was only one way he could have known about the murder. And that was if he…

Clack.

Bonnie's mind was racing, but a sound that she had been ignoring was now approaching the study door. Clack-clack-clack.

Herman Hornville was returning. Bonnie was trapped.

"But, Father!" came Dana's voice loudly from outside the door.

"In a moment, Dana; I must take this call," said a muffled Mr Hornville.

"Cock-a-doodle…"

Bonnie did not even have time to panic. As the study door swung open, she dived into the kneehole under Herman Hornville's desk and scrunched herself down as small as she could go.

"…doo," finished Dana pathetically.

236

Mr Hornville strode into the study distractedly, talking on his mobile.

It was one thing to sneak around Harriet Spruce's house as the great detective Montgomery Bonbon. Being caught here – a little girl in the local bigwig's study – would be so much worse. Bonnie had visions of being pulled out from under the desk by the scruff of her neck and tossed out onto the pavement. The little grey man in the lift would love that.

"No, Harriet… No, I understand… I am listening," said Mr Hornville. Bonnie could hear him circling the room. He seemed to be looking for something.

"I know you would never hurt the museum, Harriet. I know," he said wearily, "but I rather think your one phone call should have been to a lawyer…"

Dana's father rummaged through the desk drawers next to Bonnie. She closed her eyes and tried to shrink. She tried to think tiny thoughts. Dried peas. Advent calendar chocolates. Her interest in sport.

"Listen, I'll make a call to the museum's solicitors, Morecambe, Morecambe and Wise. Yes, of course. Don't worry, I'll do it right now."

He ended the call with a long sigh. Bonnie risked opening one eye slightly. He was patting his pockets and rapping his fingers on his desk. It was interesting to observe someone who did not know he was being observed. Herman Hornville, who had seemed so intimidating and austere when she first saw him in the museum, was now singing a little song under his breath.

"Address booook, address booook, where are you? Hallooo? Aha!"

An idea seemed to strike, and Mr Hornville made directly for the centre of the bookcase. Bonnie risked the tiniest of peeks from behind the desk. At first she thought that the museum owner was looking for his address book among the other tomes. Then she saw something that almost made her gasp.

Part of Herman Hornville's bookcase began to move. Part of his bookcase began to *turn*.

Bonnie could hardly believe it. But of course, it all made sense. What was the point of being rich if you did not spend your money on cool stuff like revolving bookcases?

He disappeared through the open bookcase, then reappeared a moment later holding a small leather-bound book. His *address* book, deduced Bonnie, as Herman Hornville allowed the bookcase to slide neatly, almost silently, back into place.

A loud knock came from the study door.

"Father? Father!" called Dana's voice from outside.

Mr Hornville opened the door.

"I was trying to show you something! In the … living room," said Dana, looking very stressed.

"Dana, I'm in the middle of something."

"But you work so hard. I wanted to give you a

chance to get out," said Dana with all the subtlety of an antelope wearing clogs.

"Well," mused Herman Hornville, "I suppose Ms Spruce isn't going anywhere. What were you saying?"

He followed Dana out of the study, and Bonnie breathed out for what felt like the first time that day. She knew she had to do what Dana said – get out. But Montgomery Bonbon was in there with her, and he could not possibly leave without investigating Herman Hornville's secret.

She sprang from of her hiding place and planted herself exactly where Mr Hornville had stood when he opened the bookcase. If Bonnie knew anything about bookcases that spin around, she knew they were always opened by pulling a certain special book. The question was, which one? She could hardly look for fingerprints in the dust. There was no dust.

Dana's father was a lot taller than Bonnie, so she stretched up on her toes and craned her neck to see the books that were nearer his level. There it was! It had to be. A book entitled *Unlocking the Shelf.* Bonnie pulled at the spine…

And nothing happened.

When she looked again, she realized that the book was in fact called *Unlocking the Self: Five Steps to Being a Youier You*.

Drat! She was running out of time. Her eyes flitted across the spines and lit on a music book called *Hidden Handel*. She pulled it.

Again, nothing.

And then she saw it. A book in French. It had – it absolutely *had* – to be the right one: *Le Secret d'Or*.

She pulled at the spine of *Le Secret d'Or*, and, with the gentlest of purring sounds, Herman Hornville's hidden door began to open.

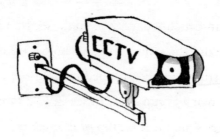

Chapter Twenty-Two

What the Squirrelephant Saw

"*Bellissimo!*" Bonnie said in Montgomery Bonbon's voice. He would be pleased with that bit of detective work.

The revolving bookcase opened to reveal a dark little chamber. As she peered into the shadows, Bonnie felt a tickling sensation in her throat. For a moment, she thought she was going to cough. Was that… Was that *dust*? Crossing the threshold, she realized she was stepping into what had once been the chimney of a large fireplace. The tapering walls stretched up, up past the ceiling of Mr Hornville's study, all the way to the roof.

When Bonnie's room got so messy her mum could not stand it any longer, Bonnie would simply lob all her junk into a cupboard. She could see that Herman Hornville did the same thing: a whole lifetime's worth of stuff had been heaped into this tiny space, where no one was supposed to see it. Old books and newspapers were piled on top of dilapidated board games and an open packet of dusty wine gums. The secret room was illuminated by the flickering blue-white glow of half a dozen screens, stacked on top of one another.

The CCTV cameras. Herman Hornville's third eye. Bonnie – and Dana – had been right.

She inched further into the half-light, listening to the monitors' electric hum. Every screen was a black and white window into a different room at the museum. It was as if the Hornville itself had been cut up and put on display in glass cases. The rooms were all empty; the museum was still closed, by order of Inspector Sands. A bored-looking police officer patrolled the vacant rooms, disappearing from one screen and reappearing in the next.

Bonnie craned her neck to get a better look, leaning on what she thought was a small desk, and suddenly the police officer began moving backwards. She swept away some ancient crisp packets, uncovering an old-fashioned control panel with a chunky plastic dial in the middle.

She turned the dial to the right, and the officer started plodding forward once again. She turned it to the left, and they zipped around the museum in reverse. She turned it further and the images rewound faster and faster, until the figure was a blur. Bonnie watched the Hornville get darker and then brighter, darker and brighter as she travelled backwards in time. This was exactly what she needed to find out what really happened to Oliver Munday.

She whizzed and whizzed, willing the dial to whizz faster until – all at once – the screens turned pitch-black. She had rewound all the way to the power cut on the day of the murder.

She spun the dial a little to the right and the screens fizzed back to life. She paused the recording, leaning in closer to the monitor labelled 6. The one showing the turret room. There, hovering in front of Bonnie's nose, frozen in time, was a scene she recognized. There was the empty pedestal. There was

Oliver Munday, lying dead on the floor. There were Anton, Harriet and Rashida, along with Grampa Banks and Montgomery Bonbon.

A stray thought crept in from the corner of Bonnie's brain. *Is that what my moustache looks like?*

And there was Inspector Sands, who seemed to be pointing directly at the hidden camera. Bonnie could remember the inspector saying, "Are you telling me you've got a flippin' massive squirreffelant but you don't have any security cameras?"

Maybe Sands did have a few very basic detective instincts after all.

Bonnie held her breath and turned the dial to the left. The screens went black for a moment, and then – *pop!* – the picture came back. Oliver Munday was alive, standing on duty in the turret room. The Widdlington Eagle was in its place on the pedestal. Bonnie had never seen Oliver alive, and it was odd to see this tiny, glowing version of him. He checked his watch, then looked around the room.

It went black. The power cut again. What happened in that room while the lights were out?

Bonnie rewound once more. Going back earlier, she watched visitors totter in and out of the turret room. She saw Anton Price wheeling his squeaky cleaning trolley and dusting the exhibit. She saw Rashida Zaki leading a tour group around the pedestal. And she saw the room empty, apart from Oliver Munday and the Widdlington Eagle.

Then black.

The video showed nothing. No thief. No Blowpipe Killer. Nothing.

Bonnie had to have missed something. She wiped dust from the screen, hoping that another viewing would reveal more. In doing so, her sleeve caught the screen's paper label, sending the number *6* fluttering off towards Bonnie's feet like a sycamore seed.

She bent down to pick it up. Where she expected to see the number *6*, she found the number *9* staring back up at her. Of course, the label was simply upside down.

Of course.

When Bonnie found two enigmatic scraps of paper on the Hornville Museum's roof, she had been looking for a clever explanation. Grampa Banks had suggested a code or a map reference. It was the simplest thing in the world: she had been looking at the problem upside down. The scraps of paper did not read *61* and *1E*. They read *19* and *31*: 1931, the year the Widdlington Eagle was sold.

An idea began to form in Bonnie's mind.

The dust on Oliver Munday's cuffs…

The impossible photograph of Eudora Potts…

And the phantom thief who nobody saw, not even the squirrelephant…

That's it, thought Bonnie. That's really it! It's the only thing that makes sense. So the murderer is—

"Busted," said Herman Hornville.

Bonnie had not noticed the study door open. She swivelled on the spot to see Dana, racked with guilt, and her father, stormy-faced. All Dana could manage was a small, apologetic, "Cock-a-doodle-doo!"

Mr Hornville ducked into the secret room, his brow so knitted he could have been making a scarf. He towered over Bonnie for a second, and then flumped down onto a box of old magazines like a deflating bouncy castle.

"I'm very, very sorry about all this," he said, waving a hand towards the screens. His voice knocked Bonnie off-kilter for a moment. Mr Hornville did not sound like he was brimming with rage. He sounded like he was brimming with … sad?

"I – I know I should have told everyone about the cameras. There was just … never a good time. I knew if you ever came in here, you'd rumble the whole thing, Dana. You've always been too smart for me."

He turned to Bonnie. "I'm sorry you were dragged into this, Ms Montgomery. I don't blame you for going along with my daughter's scheme. It's obvious from looking at you that you don't have the intelligence to mastermind a caper like this."

"But…" Bonnie began, then caught her words before they left her lips. It was better, she realized, if Mr Hornville believed this was all Dana's idea.

"Thank you," she managed.

"No need to apologize!" said Mr Hornville loftily. "I am the one who owes everyone an apology. I should have told the police about the cameras right away. But they didn't show anything, you must understand. One minute the eagle was there, and the next … it wasn't. One minute poor Oliver was alive, and the next…"

He buried his face in his hands. Dana patted him on the head. Bonnie got the impression the Hornvilles were not huggers.

"Perhaps that detective will find a clue in the video?" suggested Dana.

Her father drew himself up and took a deep breath. "Yes, yes. You're right. I shall telephone Inspector Sands immediately."

"Actually, I was thinking of that other detective," said Dana. "What's his name? Mountbatten Yumyum?"

"Montgomery Bonbon!" burst out Bonnie, before adding, "I think."

"Either way," said Mr Hornville with a long sigh, "it looks like the cheese tasting is cancelled."

Behind her father, Dana mouthed a silent, "Yesssss!"

Bonnie knew how Dana felt, although she had no strong feelings about the cheese tasting being cancelled. Bonnie felt a thrill of triumph because she had finally solved the murder in the museum.

Chapter Twenty-Three

The Denouement

The sign on the main entrance to the Hornville Museum read: *Closed for Denouement*. Bonnie had painted it herself. It had taken her three tries to get the *nouem* right.

According to the very last entry in *A Detective's Dictionary* (1968), the word *denouement* means the part of a mystery where the detective reveals the murderer. Even alphabetical order has to take a back seat when it comes to denouements: they always have to come at the end. Suspects must be gathered together. Mysteries must be unravelled. Traps must be sprung.

It was very hard to spell *denouement*, and it was even harder to pronounce the word. But pulling off a successful denouement? That was the hardest thing of all. Bonnie was going to need help.

Following the discovery of Herman Hornville's secret yesterday, Grampa Banks had handwritten and delivered five messages that read:

YOUR PRESENCE IS REQUESTED IN THE
HORNVILLE MUSEUM STOREROOM
AT 11AM SHARP TOMORROW
WHEREUPON OLIVER MUNDAY'S KILLER SHALL BE
REVEALED. MONTGOMERY BONBON,
DETECTIVE (GREAT)

Now, as clocks throughout the museum warbled, clucked and chimed eleven, Bonnie joined her loyal assistant in the storeroom. She had not been in there since the night of the intruder. Even with the lights on, the windowless room was cramped and oppressive. Grampa Banks was rocking back and forth on the soles of his ever so polished shoes and twisting a handkerchief between his fingers. Bonnie could tell he was anxious.

"Are you sure this'll work, old chap?" he asked. "What if the one who did it doesn't turn up?"

Bonnie did her utmost to radiate confidence. She planted her feet and stood bolt upright in Montgomery Bonbon's raincoat. Bonbon's moustache bristled on her upper lip. It was good to be back.

"Please do not discompose yourself, *mein ami*," she said in Bonbon's most reassuring tone. "Our killer has the most excellent reason to be joining us."

This seemed to relax Grampa Banks a little. He mopped the back of his neck with his handkerchief and tucked it away just before their guests began to arrive.

"All right, this better be good," said Inspector Sands, stomping up to Bonnie. "I'm a copper and it's eleven in the flippin' morning. I'm normally in bed. What's a *den-ooie-ment*, anyway?"

"*Day-noo-mon*," corrected Bonnie.

The inspector was followed by Constable Simon, who was carrying a roll of paper in one hand; the other was handcuffed to a droopy-looking Harriet Spruce. Much like one of her plants, she seemed to be wilting in police custody. Anton Price shuffled in behind Harriet, glancing nervously in her direction. Then came Rashida Zaki, putting on a show of indifference that Bonnie could see straight through. Herman Hornville crept in last. His shoes did not even make a *clack-clack-clack*.

The guests arranged themselves awkwardly in the storeroom, glancing around the crowded space in trepidation. Herman Hornville and Inspector Sands found a couple of stools; Rashida leaned against a filing cabinet; Anton wheeled over his cleaning trolley – *squeak-squeak-squawk* – and perched on it. They all stared expectantly at Montgomery Bonbon.

"Well?" demanded Inspector Sands, snacking noisily on a packet of salty nuts.

Bonnie cleared her throat. "Who killed Oliver Munday?" she asked theatrically.

"Ooh, I know this one!" cried Sands, pointing a finger excitedly in the direction of Harriet Spruce. "She did!"

Bonnie had a horrible feeling that Inspector Sands had decided a denouement was some kind of quiz. She cleared her throat again.

"Permit me to remind you, Inspecteur, that we have been seeking not only your so-called Blowpipe Killer, but also the individual you named the *inside man*."

"Or person," chipped in Inspector Sands.

"Quite."

Bonnie began to pace around the storeroom slowly. "In fact, the killer did have such an accomplice. And the identity of this accomplice is known to Montgomery Bonbon."

"Do you want to make it known to Inspector bloomin' Sands?"

"Very well!" Bonnie turned sharply, and the whole room seemed to breathe in. "The killer's accomplice was none other than…" She wiggled the moustache. "Oliver Munday!"

The delicious sound of confusion spread around the room. Heads were shaken; brows were furrowed; eyes were squinted.

"But he were the one what *died*! How could he be the killer's accomplice?" the inspector spluttered.

Bonnie put a finger to her lips and raised one

eyebrow. "From the beginning of this most puzzling case, the question to Montgomery Bonbon was clear: what happened in the turret room when the lights, they went out?"

One by one, she fixed each person with an unflinching gaze. "One person in this room knows the answer to that question."

"All right, I admit it!" groaned Herman Hornville, throwing his hands up in the air. Gasps of astonishment rippled around the storeroom. "There's a hidden camera in the turret room. There are hidden cameras all over the museum!"

"Mr Hornville!" cried Harriet Spruce indignantly.

"You flaming ... WHAT?" fumed Inspector Sands. "Are you telling me that this place had CCTV all along and you never told us?" She looked around the room in disbelief. "I could nick the whole lot of you for wasting police time! I could! I could... I need to sit down."

"You are sitting down, Inspector," muttered Grampa Banks.

"Then I..." She looked like she was about to burst into flames. "Then I've half a mind..."

"You can say that again," murmured Bonnie.

"Forgive me, Inspector," said Herman Hornville. "Forgive me, all of you. I sent the recordings from the turret room to the police station yesterday afternoon. But – I swear! – they didn't show anything. One minute poor Oliver was alive; the next…"

"Why haven't I heard about this, Simon?" Inspector Sands really was on her feet now, bearing down on the young constable. Her face looked like you could fry an egg on it.

"I thought you knew, ma'am. Th – that was the impression I got from Mr Banks. He caught me outside the station and asked me to print this." The constable unrolled his large sheet of paper.

"What the heck is that? A spot the difference?"

"It's a printout, ma'am. Of the crime scene before and after the power cut. Look, here's Mr Munday before and … erm … after."

Inspector Sands squinted hard at the fuzzy images. "What, no bandit with a blowpipe?"

"No, ma'am."

"Then what's the bloomin' point of wasting all

that printer ink? And since when do my officers run errands for civilians, Constable?"

"Well, it seemed like the least I could do after Mr Banks dropped off all those crisps and that packet of salty nuts."

Inspector Sands swiftly crumpled the now empty packet into her back pocket.

Bonnie knew she had to wrestle the denouement under control. She stepped deftly between Inspector Sands and the printout.

"To understand these images," Bonnie continued dramatically, "we must to be travelling backwards in time. Almost one hundred years."

"Well, hurry it up," grumbled the inspector, dropping back onto her stool. "I've a meeting with the Lord Mayor at two, and I want to arrive before he eats all the fondant fancies."

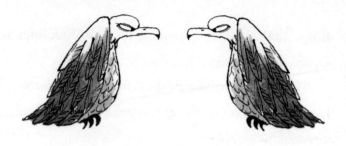

Chapter Twenty-Four
Whodunit?

"Rashida Zaki." Bonnie swung a finger around to point at the museum guide, who almost slipped off the cabinet she was leaning on. "Or should I call you Madison Garden? You are researching a podcast about the Widdlington Eagle, *non*?"

"How did you—?"

Bonnie smiled smugly. "Montgomery Bonbon, he knows all."

Rashida hissed a curse at whichever rival podcast the kid in the graveyard had leaked her story to.

"Please tell to the room what you discovered."

"Well." Rashida cleared her throat. "Everyone

thinks that Abelard Hornville found the Widdlington Eagle."

"*Well*, that's because he did," interrupted Herman Hornville, before shrinking beneath the withering glares of his employees.

"I'm afraid not, sir," replied Rashida sternly. "Sure, your granddaddy took the credit – and the money – but it was actually discovered by an employee of his named Eudora Potts. I've documented the whole thing. The proof is right there in the museum records, if you know where to look."

The Herman Hornville who had stridden into the museum on the night of the murder would have argued, Bonnie thought. He would have stood up for his family's reputation. But a humbler Herman Hornville seemed to be running the show now.

"Eudora…" repeated Dana's father. "Well, I never."

Inspector Sands was pinching the bridge of her nose, and the vein in her forehead was pulsing so hard Bonnie thought it might be considering a solo career. "Can someone make me care about this even a smidge?" she growled.

Bonnie nudged Grampa Banks. He held up the photograph he had "borrowed" from Anton Price's home and showed it to the room. The museum restorer's jaw dropped open when he saw it.

Bonnie continued. "Bonbon submits to you this most unusual photograph. The picture, you see — she is impossible. The Widdlington Eagle, it was sold in 1931, and yet it can clearly be seen here in a photograph from 1955. The eagle did not leave the New Jersey Museum for Neat Old Stuff until this year. So how to explain it? There is only one way."

"Magic!" breathed Constable Simon, instantly realizing he had made a mistake.

"There was not one Widdlington Eagle. There must have been two." Bonnie turned to Herman Hornville. "Eudora Potts, she was making sculptures, was she not?"

"Why, yes. In fact, I have a picture of her sculpting clay in my study. But how did you…?"

"Montgomery Bonbon, he knows all. Now, imagine: it is 1931. Poor Eudora Potts, she knows that her discovery is about to be snatched out of her hands. What would be more natural than to make a copy of the Widdlington Eagle, *un memento*? The treasure will be lost, *ja*, but the copy, it will stay with her."

Constable Simon was still holding the grainy black-and-white images of the turret room. Bonnie pointed to the statuette mounted on the pedestal in the centre of the "before" image. "And Montgomery Bonbon, he tells to you that the Widdlington Eagle in this picture is not the original Widdlington Eagle. *Non*. It is the *clay replica*."

"Impossible!"

"Outrageous!"

"Absurd!"

"Hold on a moment. Does this mean that the real statue was never actually stolen?" asked Harriet, unable to disguise the note of hope in her voice.

"Sadly not, Fräulein," said Bonnie. "Please to listen.

When the lights go out, that is Oliver Munday's signal. He is removing the fake, false, fabricated eagle from its case. He is taking it to the window. And he is dashing it to the little pieces among the gravel on the flat roof of the museum. That is why the victim, his cuffs were covered with the fine powder. All that remains are the torn scraps of a paper label that once read *1931* – the year the replica was made."

Bonnie held up the carefully reconstructed label. Her heart was thumping. She wondered if this was how Dana felt when she was singing a solo.

"Hold up, hold up!" Bonnie had never seen Inspector Sands concentrating so intently. "You're telling me there were *two* of the blasted things all along? Why didn't I know that?"

"Actually, guv," admitted Constable Simon sheepishly, "when we were searching the storeroom after the break-in, we did notice something in the records called the 1931 replica." He began to melt under Inspector Sands's glare. "But we didn't think it was … relevant."

Bonnie could tell Simon was not looking forward to the drive back to the police station.

"What happened next?" asked Rashida.

"Next," said Bonnie, "Oliver Munday, he uses his singer's lungs to scream the most dreadful scream. And he pretends to be dead upon the floor."

"But, Detective," said Anton, politely raising a finger, "when we found Oliver, he wasn't pretending to be dead. He was dead."

Harriet and Rashida nodded in agreement.

"I was *just* gonna say that," said Inspector Sands. "And if that palaver about the fake doodah is true, what happened to the real eagle? Flippin' flapped out the window, did it?"

"Patience! Patience, dear Inspecteur," said Bonnie in a tone of voice calculated to keep the inspector awake that night. "Now we turn to Fräulein Harriet Spruce: a woman in a financial situation most grave owing to her love of the plants."

"So what if I buy a lot of plants?" protested Harriet. "That doesn't mean I killed anyone or stole that blasted eagle, fake or otherwise. I didn't even like it!"

"And yet you owned the deadly frightshade plant which killed Oliver Munday, along with the brand-new copy of *Culpeper's Compendium*, which tells to the reader how the poison can be made."

"But I only bought that book because…" Harriet paused. Bonnie could see in her eyes that the museum's manager had started to look at this case from a different angle. The pieces were slowly coming together for her.

"Continue, *bitte*," said Bonnie.

"I bought that book because my old copy went missing. Someone must have taken it." Her eyes grew wide. "I'm being framed!"

Inspector Sands turned to Bonnie. "If Mother Nature here is so innocent, who fired the dart at Mr Corduroy over there?"

"Yes," said Anton, "who fired the dart at me?"

"That is most simple." Bonnie snapped her heels together. "You did."

Another gasp travelled around the room. Only Anton remained completely, utterly still.

Chapter Twenty-Five
J'accuse!

"This has to be a joke!" spluttered Anton. "And I don't much care for your sense of humour, Bonbon."

"A joke, *ja*. A cruel joke played by you, Monsieur Price, upon poor Oliver Munday."

There was no going back. Bonnie had to make her case. She had to prove that Anton Price was the murderer. She clasped her hands tightly behind her back to stop them trembling, took a deep breath, and addressed the room.

"*Thank you for everything,*" she began. "That is what the retirement card of Anton Price said. The card chosen by Oliver Munday. I suggest to you,

Monsieur Price, that you knew young Oliver was saving money to study at the Sorbet Conservatoire. And so, you offer to him this little job. You will pay to him a fee in exchange for helping you to steal the Widdlington Eagle."

"Nonsense. Pure nonsense," scoffed Anton.

"You instruct Oliver Munday to stage the scene of the theft and then to tell the little lie about a burglar who came in the window and bopped him on the head, *ja*? Who knows how much money you promised him? Who knows when you decided that it would be safer – and cheaper – to kill him? Monsieur Oliver was a singer, *non*? And you wished to be certain that he would not *sing* to the police."

Anton made a sound like a wounded whoopee cushion.

"You planned to be with Fräulein Spruce and Mademoiselle Zaki when you found Oliver lying on the floor, as you knew he would be. You made certain that you were the one holding the torch. And this torch, you keep pointing it into the eyes of the two witnesses."

"That's right, you did! I could hardly see a thing,"

said Harriet animatedly, stepping forward and yanking Constable Simon by his cuffed wrist.

"And while your colleagues, they were dazzled, you placed the poisoned dart in Oliver Munday's neck. Only in that instant could he have known that the Anton Price he believed to be his friend had betrayed him. A crime most terrible. Most unspeakable. Most … tabloidesque."

Anton scowled. "Absolute poppycock. You must be off your rocker, Bonbon."

"You placed the dart in the victim's neck, just like you placed the dart in your own armchair. It was not fired through the window, as you wished for us to believe. You merely dropped your teapot and … twung it."

"*Twung* it?" repeated Anton with an incredulous snort. "I *twung* the dart?!"

Bonnie gave Grampa Banks a nod. He slid the end of a metal ruler off the edge of a cabinet.

"You twung it," repeated Bonnie, deadly serious, and Grampa Banks twung the end of the ruler. The storeroom was filled with a most fartiferous twong, reverberating around the stacks.

"I can't believe you're all listening to this bilge!" Anton looked round the storeroom at the others. "I suppose I caused the power cut too, did I? Would you mind explaining how I could possibly have done that?"

"*Avec* pleasure. Banks, would you mind?"

Grampa Banks swelled with pride. "This," he said with a nervous wobble in his voice, "is an ordinary kettle." He stepped aside to reveal the old kettle that Warboys the caretaker had shown them, resting on the filing cabinet behind him. "Well, it's a faulty kettle, actually. Dodgy wiring. And that got me thinking. Well, I say thinking – it actually came to me in a *dream*—"

Bonnie coughed loudly.

"The point is, switching this kettle on could blow a fuse. In an old building like this, it'd be lights out. Good old Warboys, she knew that, so she took it off for repairs. But on the day of the murder, some cheeky so-and-so went into her workshop and swiped it."

"Someone," Bonnie continued, "who wanted to cause a power cut while making a cup of tea in the staffroom."

"Oh, please." Anton rolled his eyes. "What makes you think I did that?"

"Simply, Monsieur Price, because the hidden cameras, they show you retrieving the broken kettle and installing it in the staffroom."

This was a risk. Bonnie hoped it would pay off.

"Oh, ho ho ho." Anton brightened up very suddenly. "You've blown it now, Bonbon."

Bonnie had seen Anton smile before, but never with his teeth. His waxy face seemed to change completely. His smile was so wide, so false, so mirthless.

"The so-called great detective is lying to you, don't you see?" Anton asked the room.

"What makes you think that Montgomery Bonbon, he is lying?" Bonnie demanded.

"Because there can't be footage of *anyone* moving the kettle. The cameras are inside Hornville's Monsters. That means there is no CCTV in Warboys's workshop. Or the staffroom!"

Anton looked triumphant for a moment. Then his face dropped, and Bonnie turned to the room.

"To carry out such a crime without being observed in the act even once, the murderer could only have been someone who had worked here for so long that they had learned precisely where Monsieur Hornville's security cameras were."

"Ah – well, no!" stammered Anton.

"Anton, how could you?" said Harriet.

Bonnie was starting to enjoy herself. "Therefore the killer had to be someone with a deep connection to the Hornville Museum."

Bonnie thought again of Rashida's words in the churchyard. The museum guide said that she had interviewed "Eudora's last living relative, Anton Price…" At the time, Bonnie had assumed that Eudora's last living relative and Anton Price were two separate people.

"Mademoiselle Zaki, did you interview Monsieur Price for your podcast?"

"Uh, yeah. Sure I did."

"Please to tell us why."

"Because he's Eudora Potts's grandson."

"Really?" asked Harriet.

"I knew that," said Herman Hornville.

"Which one is Eudora again?" muttered Inspector Sands.

"In fact," Bonnie continued, "the 1955 photograph shows one Maisie Potts and one Gilbert Price. Anton Price's parents, perhaps?"

"Yes, yes, that's all true," admitted Anton, "but it's no secret."

"But there *was* a secret, was there not? The secret that poor Eudora Potts, she discovered the Widdlington Eagle. The secret that meant" – Bonnie took a step towards Anton – "Abelard Hornville's fortune should have been hers. Would have been *yours*! You must have looked every day upon Monsieur Herman Hornville with his beautiful home and his wonderful museum and felt such *rage*."

Anton's lip began to curl.

Bonnie leaned in and whispered, "You bided your time, until one day – what is this? Oh! The Widdlington Eagle, she is returning at last. A chance, *non*? A chance to take back what should always have been yours!"

"I don't have to listen to this tripe. Why would I have bothered coming here today if I had that bally eagle? Wouldn't I be off on a cruise somewhere, enjoying my retirement?"

"I am certain that was being the plan, Monsieur," said Bonnie breezily. "Had it not been for Bonbon, you would have – how do you say it? – made away with the goods when you broke into this very storeroom mere hours after you killed Oliver Munday. Ah, but then the Inspecteur Sands, she so wisely places a police guard upon the door. And your retirement, it is delayed a little longer."

"You don't need to remind everyone how wise I am," said Inspector Sands, obviously delighted. "But if he swapped the eagles and took the real one, when did he do it? And where the flippin' heck is it?"

"Constable Simon, if you please?" said Bonnie.

With a little squeak of excitement, Constable Simon flipped over the printout he was holding. On the other side was a third image from the turret-room camera, showing a very fuzzy Anton Price cleaning the Widdlington Eagle.

"*Regardez!*" said Bonnie.

"Just what am I supposed to be *regardez*-ing?" snarled Anton. "You can't see anything incriminating in that picture."

"*Non*, indeed," admitted Bonnie. "You were too clever for that. On the morning of the murder, you entered the room with your cleaning trolley. Oliver Munday, he stood at the door and made sure you were not disturbed." She tapped the paper to show where Oliver had stood. "Using your knowledge of the room's secret camera, you positioned yourself between the camera and the Widdlington Eagle." She tapped the fuzzy image of Anton standing in front of the pedestal. "To the viewer you appear to be dusting the exhibit. In fact, you are exchanging the replica for the real eagle."

"Can you actually see him doing any of that?" whispered Inspector Sands to Bonnie.

"Well … *non*."

The inspector winced. "He's going to get away with this, isn't he?"

"Oh, this is rich!" said Anton with a grin that said, "I'm going to get away with this, aren't I?" He raised an eyebrow. "Do you have pictures of me *not* committing any other crimes? Not stealing the crown jewels, perhaps? Maybe I *didn't* assassinate the Latvian ambassador while I was at it?"

If Anton had been any more gleeful, he would have been rubbing his hands.

"Erm…" stammered Bonnie.

Six faces turned towards her. No one had heard Montgomery Bonbon say *erm* before. Montgomery Bonbon did not *erm*. Montgomery Bonbon, he knew all. *Erming* was off the table.

Grampa Banks stepped in. "Look… Listen, folks… Let's calm down a little. Why don't I make us all a nice cup of tea?"

He turned to put the kettle on, and the rest of the room seemed to move in slow motion. Rashida clapped her hands to her cheeks. Herman Hornville looked like he was about to tug the triangular beard clean off his face. Harriet stretched out her arm, yanking Constable Simon off balance.

"*Non!*" shouted Bonnie.

But it was too late. Grampa Banks's finger flicked the kettle's switch and…

Poomf!

The lights went out.

Chapter Twenty-Six

A Light in the Dark

The windowless storeroom swam with inky blackness. *Crash!* **CLATTER!** *Squeak!* Shrieks filled the darkness, and loudest among the shouts was the voice of Montgomery Bonbon.

"Nobody to move!"

With her moustache invisible, Bonnie's words did not have their usual impact.

"Simon, get to the fuse box!" commanded Inspector Sands.

"I've fallen over, ma'am. Ms Spruce appears to be sitting on me."

It was pandemonium. Bonnie could hear people

clambering over one another, clonking into filing cabinets and rattling shelves.

"I'm so, so sorry, everyone," said Grampa Banks. "I'll have the lights back on in ten minutes."

"Ten minutes?!" said Inspector Sands. "That's no flippin' good; we need the lights back on right—"

VWOOM!

As quickly as they went out, the lights came back on. Everyone looked shocked, apart from Bonnie and Grampa Banks. The warm, open face of Warboys appeared from behind the storeroom door.

"I replaced the fuse, Mr Bonbon, Mr Banks. Did it work out like you planned?"

"Precisely, Warboys." Bonnie smiled under her moustache. "Most excellent work."

Bonnie was looking at Anton Price. Everyone was looking at Anton Price. He was crouched on the ground, like an old dead spider, wrapped up in his own spindly legs. In front of him was his cleaning trolley, the one Bonnie had seen him *squeak-squeak-squawking* around the museum. The one he had been wheeling in the security camera footage. The one Bonnie had hidden next to, that night in the storeroom. The one that had been *locked*.

Between his bony finger and thumb Anton held a small key, poised over the lock: he had frozen stiff the moment the lights had come back on.

"Monsieur Price, perhaps you would show to Inspecteur Sands what is inside the cleaning trolley you were so keen to open under cover of darkness?" said Bonnie.

Anton growled something under his breath.

"Gerrit open, now," said Inspector Sands. It was not a request.

Anton reluctantly slid the key into the lock and, with a twist and a click, the trolley door swung open. Inside sat a bundle of yellow dust cloths, a tin of brass polish, a dustpan and a brush.

And, of course, the Widdlington Eagle.

The key dropped from Anton's fingers, and he slumped to the ground.

"I misjudged you, Monsieur Price," said Bonnie truthfully. "You, with your quiet manners and your old photographs. Bonbon, he thinks to himself, here is a man who truly loves the museum. A man who is proud of his work. But *non*. To destroy your grandmother's beautiful sculpture like you smash her teapot. *Non*. I do not believe there is any love left inside you. Only the bitterness."

"Very clever, you revolting little man," sneered Anton.

Bonnie could almost hear Inspector Sands wriggling her toes inside her boots. She thought the inspector was gearing up to say, "You're nicked," but instead she turned to Bonnie.

"Go on," she said grudgingly, "you say it, Bonbon. You're a blasted menace, but you earned it."

Montgomery Bonbon puffed up his chest, and with a flourish said, "You are being nicked, mate."

Epilogue

It was a very unusual evening at St Hilaria's Church of the Unfounded Assumption. Bonnie glanced down at the programme in her hands:

Montgomery Bonbon had been unable to attend, so Bonnie Montgomery had come along as Grampa Banks's guest. They were sitting at the back, and the music was so beautiful that the attendees hardly noticed how uncomfortable the pews were. At least, no one had said anything about it. Even Inspector Sands was not complaining for once.

Bonnie felt a great sense of relief. If it had not been for Montgomery Bonbon, the killer would never have been caught. Without Grampa Banks – without her mum, even – she might never have been able to piece the whole thing together and poor Harriet Spruce would have been done for: an innocent oddball might never have seen her beloved plants again.

And yet, Bonnie knew that the satisfaction of solving a case was always tinged with sadness. You could not solve a murder case without a murder victim, after all.

Perhaps it was the singing, perhaps it was Dana's voice, but Bonnie could feel her nose getting red and her eyes beginning to blur when she remembered that Oliver Munday would never sing again.

She blinked away a tear or two and when her vision cleared, she saw something unexpected. Someone had dropped an envelope onto the empty seat beside her.

Bonnie Montgomery was written on it in glittery purple pen. How long had it been there? Bonnie looked around, but there was no sign of the person who had left it. Everyone else seemed to be engrossed in the performance.

With a finger, Bonnie carefully opened the envelope and pulled out a small sheet of thick, cream-coloured paper. As she unfolded it, her thoughts seemed to drown out the music. She could hear her heart beating in her ears. For a moment, it felt as if the very foundations of the church were quaking.

The note bore only two words.

AUTHOR'S NOTE

Thank you for reading all the way to the end of my book. Unless you are one of those people who skip to the end first, to find out what happens. If that is the case:

IN THE END, THE WHALE KILLED EVERYONE APART FROM ISHMAEL.

That's the end of Moby Dick. I just saved you seven hundred pages.

Montgomery Bonbon: Murder at the Museum is my first book, so go easy on me, please. I am grateful to all the great mystery writers whose works I have so scurrilously plundered for this volume.

I would also like to thank my editor, Gráinne; as well as my personal apothecary, Sven Vest; my life coach, Nancy Vest (no relation); my ostler, Alan Mice; my mouse, Alan (no relation); and my parents, Xanu and The Great Becoming. Thank you all.

Alasdair Beckett-King

Ivory Towers, 2022

MONTGOMERY BONBON'S

next case

COMING SOON